I0577966

WHERE THEIR HEARTS COLLIDE

WARDHAM BOOK 3

ZOE YORK

ZOYO PRESS

COPYRIGHT

Copyright © 2013 Zoe York
Self-published
All rights reserved.

Ingram Spark edition, 2019
ISBN-13: 978-1-926527-56-7

www.zoeyork.com

DEDICATION

can't help but love gruff men in uniform

For my husband, the gruffest of all

ABOUT THIS BOOK

When the girl next door...
Karen's finally decided what she wants to do when she grows up.
Too bad it'll mean leaving behind her new neighbour, who's
stirred up a different kind of grown up feelings. But when he
rebuffs her attempt to have a fling before she leaves Wardham,
Karen knows it's for the best. A clean break, no messy emotional
entanglements.

Meets the cop of her dreams...
Intense and private, Paul has recently moved to Wardham for a
more family friendly job, leaving behind a career as a homicide
detective in the city. He only has his ten year old daughter a few
nights a week, and he doesn't want any distractions or drama
while he tries to repair their relationship.

At exactly the wrong time.
But Karen is right next door, and everywhere he goes. His resolve
to keep his distance only lasts until she needs a true friend in her
corner, and he realizes he can't imagine life without her.

———

1

———

IT was a shame the guy next door was so rude. If he smiled, he'd probably be drop-dead gorgeous. If he smiled, that might mean she finally had his attention.

Karen peeked out the corner of her eye at the post-war bungalow on the other side of her driveway. The *shared* driveway. A mirror image of her house, with dark red brick and pretty white trim. A wide front porch—his was bare, except for a broom. Hers had her beloved bicycle in a place of honour, and a comfortable wicker conversation set decorated with navy cushions.

Between their houses sat his sensible four door sedan. Now it was awkward. *Should have told him the first time.*

She'd come home from work three weeks ago to find the house next to hers no longer vacant. Her standard welcome-to-the-street spiel had died on her lips as the new resident jogged out the door and straight past her, as if she hadn't been standing next to his front walk. Technically on the sidewalk, but her intent to greet him had been clear. *Hadn't it?*

That was followed by two more non-meetings, which chafed her because she liked to be known as a friendly person. Forcing her neighbour to have a conversation crossed a line into needy.

She'd been looking for a natural opening to a conversation. Now she needed to make it happen.

April was around the corner, and her Camaro was calling to be let loose on the road. As soon as the last threat of snow passed, she'd need to use the shared driveway to get 304 horsepower of Victory Red awesomeness onto the roads. Hard to do with his fuel-efficient safetymobile in the way.

So she was killing time in her front yard, pretending to tidy her flower beds, planning the best way to ambush a stranger. Not her finest moment.

Since he'd been home all day, he was probably going to leave soon. He worked shifts, leaving either early in the morning or around dinner time, and was often gone for the better part of a day.

She felt like a stalker, but really, he hadn't left her any choice. And it's not like she'd gone through his mail or trash. She really didn't know anything about him except for his schedule and where he parked. *And that he had single-handedly increased the hot quotient of Wardham by 1000%.* She didn't even know how old he was, although she guessed around her age, maybe a little bit older. No way would a guy in his twenties drive that car.

Two bags of twigs later, because pretending to work had turned into actually gardening, his front door opened. She stood, stretching her back before moving to intercept him before he could get to his car. "Hi! You must be my new neighbour." She offered her hand before remembering she was covered in dirt, and quickly converted the gesture to a wave. "Karen Miller."

He nodded, and stepped around her to put his duffle bag in the trunk.

"So, there was something I wanted to talk to you about, if you can spare a second?"

Another nod, and a raised eyebrow.

Karen paused a beat, then continued. "The driveway. It's actually a shared lane."

He glanced between their houses, then to his car, and finally back to her. He might not be big on words, but he wasn't shy about looking at her. He didn't seem shy at all, actually. She couldn't put her finger on it, but something about his appraisal seemed like a power play.

She bristled. "Look, your landlord should have explained this, and I'm sorry, but my car is in—"

"I bought it." His voice was quiet and calm, the opposite of his gaze. An unsettling combination.

"I'm sorry?"

"The house. I don't have a landlord."

"It wasn't for sale. I'd have seen a sign." It didn't matter, but something made her want to argue the point just because.

"Private sale."

"Well, okay, then your agent should have told you. It's a shared drive. My car is in the garage, and I'll need to—"

"My garage is full of junk."

So? "I need—"

"I'm busy until the weekend, but I can clear it out on Saturday. Sorry about the inconvenience." And with that, he turned to get into his car.

She knew she should let it go, but his quiet tone and half-listening had frayed her nerves. "You know, the interrupting is really rude."

———

PAUL LET his lips twitch slightly before he turned to face his feisty neighbour. He hadn't meant to be rude, but he could see how she'd interpret his words that way. "That wasn't my intention, I apologize." He leaned back against his car. He had a few minutes before he had to leave, and this might be fun. "I'm out of practice on being neighbourly."

She relaxed and slid her hands into the back pockets of her jeans, streaking dirt across her left hip. A curvy, round hip he had no business noticing, but she was right in front of him. With him slouched back against the car, they were almost the same height. He liked that she was tall. Too bad he wasn't interested in dating, or any other recreational activities, because there was a lot to like about this woman. Her sass, for one. Yeah, he really liked that. He grinned, and she rewarded him with a smile that bordered on sheepish.

"I'm sorry, too. You're obviously on your way somewhere, and I've just tossed this information at you."

"It's okay, I've got a minute. Why hasn't this come up before?" He knew that she walked or biked to work, although he hadn't figured out where that was. In a few more weeks, he'd probably know a lot more about her, and most of the other citizens of Wardham, but right now he was still commuting to the city.

"I don't drive much in the winter."

That explained the bicycle. Maybe she wasn't comfortable in the snow. "Do you have people who can pick you up when it's really cold?"

"What?" She wrinkled her brow, which was really cute, even for someone who was afraid of driving. Paul didn't usually have time for that kind of weakness, but he'd probably make an exception for his new neighbour. When a look of horror crossed her face, he realized belatedly that he probably wasn't going to get a chance to offer his assistance. "You think I'm afraid of snow? Or driving in general?"

Instead of being offended, she burst out in a beautiful peal of laughter that expanded until it encompassed him and he was chuckling along with her. "No? That's not...?"

"No." She smiled and leaned forward, as if to share a conspiratorial secret. "I drive a Camaro. It's my baby, and I have snow tires, but really, it's not built for winter driving."

Oh crap. Paul could see an entirely different encounter in their near future. Instead of offering to help with her errands, he was going to be writing her speeding tickets. "It's not?"

"Of course not. Some people love that thrill, rear-wheel drive, you know, but I'm all about the straight up speed. Dry road, warm summer day."

Damn. "Listen, Karen..."

"Yeah?" Her smile was wide and happy, and about to disappear.

"I need to finish introducing myself."

"Why? What are you, a cop or something?"

"Yes."

She blinked once, and twice, then her eyes got big and round and her hand slapped over her mouth. "Oh shit!"

He was about to apologize, for what he wasn't sure, when she started laughing again. He was quickly figuring out that she did that a lot. He liked it. Which was as good a reason as any to make his goodbyes and escape.

She breathed a contented sigh and stepped back, as if she sensed he needed to leave. He liked that too. "Okay, Constable. I look forward to sharing the driveway, and the roads around Wardham, with you, at a reasonable and posted speed."

His lips quirked and he nodded brusquely to cover up. He had the funny feeling that Karen Miller could quickly get under his skin, and giving her any opening was just asking for trouble. Good trouble, but he wasn't in the market for that, or anything else. "Sounds good. I'll get the garage cleared out on the weekend."

He watched her saunter back up her front steps and lean over to collect gardening gear. His gaze lingered on her ass, until he forced himself to get in the car and drive away.

———

"There's a new sheriff in town."

Karen's best friend Carrie glanced up from behind the espresso machine. "Did we have an old sheriff?"

"You know what I mean."

"You have gossip about the new guy at the Wardham detachment?"

"Maybe. What do you know?" Karen slid onto a barstool. A Bun In The Oven didn't have tables, but three stools lived in front of the espresso bar for just these kinds of conversations.

Carrie laughed. "Not much, other than the position has been filled and the new person's going to start in a couple of weeks. He works in Windsor right now."

That would explain the weird hours. "The new person is Hot Neighbour."

"The rude guy?"

Karen shrugged. "He's a bit brusque, but I wouldn't say he's rude."

"You said he was rude yesterday. And twice last week."

"That was before I actually talked to him."

Carrie cocked an eyebrow.

"I stopped him today and asked him to start parking in his garage."

"Did you explain it was because of your *need for speed?*" Her friend giggled at the thought. It was true, though. In the summer, as often as she could find time, Karen headed out along the lake with the windows down. Alone with the wind and her music, it was hard to be 100% mindful of the speed limit.

"It came up. Before I knew he was a cop. It's not like I'm a criminal."

"No, but you like to drive fast enough that he'd need to pull you over. Of course, maybe that would be okay. Maybe he'd get you to step out of the car so he could frisk you."

"For a traffic stop? You've got issues." Although Karen couldn't deny that she'd enjoy being patted down by Paul. And interrogated. She shivered at the image of him leaning over a table at her, pinning her down with an inscrutable gaze.

Her friend pushed a latte and an orange cranberry biscotti across the bar. Fancy coffee still felt like a special treat in their sleepy little town. Karen grinned and dunked the hard biscuit.

"Mmmmm. Oh my god, this is so good." She slurped a drip of coffee from her fingertips and waved off the previous conversation. "Do we have anything to discuss before the meeting tonight?"

Carrie nodded vigorously. "Oh yes! Apparently, the funding for the new community centre is going to be approved, so we should push for agreement on what the business association is going to lobby for in terms of sponsorship and space usage. I'd love to have a chance to bid for Bun to have a coffee bar there."

"Are you ready to expand already?" Karen knew that her friend loved running her coffee shop/bakery, but she knew from first-hand experience that being an owner/operator of a store was a huge endeavour. Bun had only been open for a bit more than year.

"The centre isn't going to open next week. It'll probably be a year or two before any plans need to be implemented. And there wouldn't be any food prep there, just drinks, muffins, scones, and the like."

"Hey, you know that I've got your back. Whatever support you need, you've got it." Karen took another sip of her latte. "Is there cinnamon in this?"

Carrie nodded. "Something new I'm trying. My own simple syrups. Less sweet than the commercial bottles."

"It's good." It had cooled down enough for bigger swallows now, and before long the mug was empty. "Was good. Now gone. Hmmm. Hulk happy."

"Hey, Hulk, before you go..." Carrie pinched her lips. Karen was surprised to see her friend look so uncertain all of a sudden.

"What?"

"The community centre. The draft plans that council saw last night feature a new library."

Karen shook her head. "That's great. Isn't it?"

"It is. But someone was there from the county library service, and she was talking about getting more involved in the community. Running book clubs, that kind of thing."

"Oh." She got it now.

"You could meet with her."

"And say what? Please don't offer a professional service that interferes with my hobby?" Karen shook her head. "I don't beg."

"Who says it needs to stay a hobby?"

If only that were an option. "I have a job, remember?"

"Yeah." Her friend dumped a heaping pile of understanding in that single syllable. More than anyone else, Carrie understood family obligations. "You could talk to your parents."

If only it were that easy. "They aren't the problem."

"You sell yourself short." It was a familiar argument. Karen had supported Carrie's dream of opening Bun, and Carrie wanted to return the favour. She couldn't wrap her head around the idea that Karen was happy with her life just as it was. It would be easier to convince her if Karen still believed that to be true herself.

"I gotta go to work. See you tonight?"

Carrie pursed her lips again and nodded. Karen had almost made it out the door before her friend called out. "Hey, and don't think that's the last we've discussed of the sheriff!"

Karen laughed. As much as she'd like to fantasize otherwise, there was nothing to discuss. "Wardham doesn't have a sheriff, and I'm no librarian. Such is my lot in life."

2

———

"I SAW some kids at the park."

Paul looked up as his daughter entered the kitchen. "Sure, we could walk over there."

"Dad..." He bit back a comment on her whiny tone. "You don't need to come with me."

"Yeah, Meg, I do. For a number of reasons." He leaned back against the counter and tapped them out on his fingers. "Neither of us know this town yet, or the people here. We don't get a lot of time together, so I was hoping we could, you know, do something. Together. It's almost dinner time. And last, but definitely not least, you're only ten—"

The last point was, as he expected, the one that turned his usually agreeable daughter into a spitfire. "I'm not a little kid!"

"I know. Sweetie, I know. As much as it pains your mother and me, you are growing up. And at your mom's house, you can go to the park and walk to school by yourself because it's familiar, and people keep an eye out for you. Here...we don't know anyone yet."

"This town seems pretty safe."

He nodded. "It does. But..." Susan hated it when he used the looming threat of a boogyman, but screw it. She wasn't here and he wanted to nip the conversation in the bud. "If it was perfectly safe, I'd be out of a job. Bad people are everywhere. Okay?"

It was a good thing his daughter was easily parented, because he was pretty sure he'd make a mess of a more challenging kid. "Okay."

He pulled her into a reluctant hug and her head tucked under his chin. When did his baby get to be so tall? When did hugs become rare enough that he was just noticing where her head landed?

"Dad?"

"Mmm?"

"Can we make cookies?"

Not so big after all. "Yeah."

She giggled against his chest. "Do you even have the stuff to make cookies?"

Probably not. "Go grab the laptop and find a recipe. I've got sugar and eggs, what else do you think we'll need?"

"Uh, flour?" And the pre-teen returned in full eye-rolling force. He winced and she threw her hands in the air. "Come on, you don't have any flour?"

"What would I use it for?"

"Cookies, Dad. You'd use it to make cookies."

"I'm sorry." For not having flour? He wasn't sure that was something to be sorry about, but one thing he'd learned from his short marriage was that it was usually the right answer in situations like this. "Let's go to the store, it's a short walk."

"No." She shook her head, eyes bright. "Let's ask a neighbor. Even better plan – this way, we can meet some of those people who will watch over me when I finally get some freedom."

Before he could stop her, Megan was streaking to the front door. He trailed behind, dread and hope jockeying in his gut. Their front walk spilled onto the shared drive. Logic dictated that her first attempt at being neighbourly would be with Karen.

Maybe she wouldn't be home.

Maybe she would.

Which would he prefer? No question, he wanted to see her again. But from a distance, where he could pretend that he had room in his life for a tall, curvy drink of water with curly brown hair and eyes full of laughter. They'd only had one short conversation, but he had no problem at all imagining that spending time with Karen would be easy. Nice. *Hot.*

Really hot. On every level. Why now? Why not seven years earlier? Before he made a complete disaster of his life. Before…

"Megan, hang on." But she didn't. And he loved that about his daughter. Being fearless and friendly would serve her well in life. As an adult. Until then, he'd live in a constant state of worry.

"Don't worry, Dad. This is the done thing in small towns. It's not embarrassing." She rang Karen's doorbell, and before he could say he wasn't worried about how it looked, the door swung open.

"Yes—oh! Paul. Hi." Karen's gaze flicked up to him for a moment, then returned to Megan. "Hi. Do you live next door too? I'm Karen."

His daughter nodded. "Some of the time. I'm Megan."

The two exchanged pleasantries, and Paul stood back, struck by how similar they were. If Karen liked books, his daughter was probably going to want spend all of her time over here instead of at the park. His gut said that Karen might not mind. *There's no way you can know that.* But he did. She liked people, even him when he was curt and rude. She'd love his daughter. *Fuck.*

"…So we were hoping that maybe we could borrow some flour."

"Sure, how much?"

Megan turned and looked at him expectantly and he started. "Uh. Oh, I don't know. We hadn't gotten as far as looking up a recipe."

Karen gestured for them to step into the foyer and she moved further down the hall, raising her voice so Megan could still hear her as she headed into what was probably the kitchen. A moment later she was back, shaking her head.

"Sorry. I thought I had some, but there's barely a cup in here."

He waved off the apology. "It's okay, thank you for checking." He turned to Megan. "Let's walk to the store. It's close."

"It is," Karen interjected. "But it's also closed for the evening."

Megan groaned and Paul winced at the display. "It's okay, we'll do something else. Right? Megan?"

He had to prod her shoulder, but she nodded.

"Actually, if you want..." Karen trailed off, but laughed when Megan brightened up. She leaned toward the girl and lowered her voice conspiratorially. "I happen to have a key to the grocery store."

"You do?" Megan was breathless with excitement. So that's what it took to impress his daughter. Twenty-four hour access to cookie supplies? How about saving lives and keeping a community safe? Apparently not.

Karen nodded and grabbed a lanyard from a row of hooks on the wall. "Shall we?"

Before he could beg off, they were halfway down the block and he was left to trail behind. Which wasn't a bad place to be. His heart warmed at the sight of Megan skipping to keep up with Karen's long strides. Something else warmed as his gaze drifted to the left. Those legs. God, they went on for miles. Even in capris and boat shoes, they looked good. *She* looked good. Shapely legs, curving up to the distracting sway of her hips. Long hair swinging loose down her back. Every bit of her bouncy and happy. Strange child shows up on her doorstep? Off to the store they go to liberate a bag of flour. To make cookies.

He was doing something right. His daughter wanted to bake with him. He never thought that would happen. And that reminder was just the bucket of ice water he needed to get his mind off Karen's hips and back to the matter at hand.

He was a dad. And for a long time, he'd barely pulled his weight in that role. Because of work, and other distractions.

No more. He was here in Wardham for one reason, and one reason only. To put his daughter first.

———

KAREN LIKED KIDS. Well, she liked people, and kids were, in her experience, some of the best kind of people. Not yet jaded. Still thought they could grow up to be sports stars and fire fighters. And they could—her siblings were proof of that. Set your mind to something you love and the possibilities are endless.

She was proof of the opposite. Give up and you'd end up back at home, living your parents' dream instead.

She shook off the bitterness. It had been a long time since she'd dwelled on what could have been. It was just the rumours about the community centre that were bringing her down. It had been a week since the news broke that the library would move into the new building and expand, hire full-time staff, and offer more services. As a patron, she was excited. As someone who wanted to be a librarian a lifetime ago, she couldn't help but stifle a faint stab of jealousy at whoever would get to work in the shiny new space. Mildred Parker, who had served as Wardham's only librarian for 33 years, had made it widely known that she didn't want to work full-time, and even if she did, it sounded like the library would still be hiring new staff.

Qualified staff. Not book club hobbyists with a decade of grocery store management experience and a penchant for getting into trouble.

"Why do you have a key to the grocery store?" It had taken almost two blocks for Megan to ask this question because there were more important things to discuss first. Like how many people Karen knew down the street (at least half) and what the acceptable standard was in Wardham for kids to go to the park by themselves. The answer to this was whatever Paul wanted it to be, so she wisely guessed at eighteen and won Megan over when the girl realized it was a joke.

"Because," Karen gestured for the Reynolds to step inside after she unlocked. "This is my second home. My parents opened this store when I was a baby. I worked here all the way through high school and summers home from college. When they decided to retire, I took over as manager."

"Cool," Megan breathed.

It wasn't, exactly, but it worked. Her parents spent the winters down south, wherever her brother was playing hockey, and they came home every summer, giving her a nice long vacation so she could travel or just stay home and read. A lot. And the probably too-generous salary she earned allowed her to support that same book habit through the long winter, and share it with others through the bookmobile and book clubs she organized.

"What kind of cookies are you making?"

"Chocolate chip—"

"—Oatmeal."

Father and daughter had a nonverbal show-down for a second, but Paul backed down first. "Apparently, oatmeal chocolate chip." Megan's eyebrows shot up and he shook his head. "The oatmeal is non-negotiable, honey. It's good for your cholesterol."

Karen turned her back and headed for the baking aisle so they couldn't see her lips twisting. It was a struggle not to laugh at them, they were too cute.

And that was enough for her mind to go there. Paul. Cute. Daughter. Also cute, and she liked books.

Hot Neighbour was a single dad. That wasn't a problem at all, for her, but something told her it was an issue for him. Might explain his rudeness.

If he were anyone else, she'd just ask around, find out what the grapevine knew about him. How long had he been single. What his deal was.

But, for maybe the first time ever, she didn't want to share what she knew about him. And that's how gossip worked. A two way street of information. Or in Karen's case, she was more like the intersection of Main and Front. All information normally routed through her, at the store. Paul gossip had been sparse, though, and that made their little adventure all the more interesting. Megan had alluded to the fact that she hadn't met anyone in town yet. For tonight, they were all Karen's. As much as anyone ever was—fleetingly.

Even still, the thought gave her a little thrill.

"Everything okay?"

"Hmmm?" She turned to see father and daughter watching her with matching amused expressions.

"You've gone through a whole thing there, staring at the shelf—"

"—normally flour doesn't make people react quite so much," Megan chimed in.

Heat rushed to Karen's face, and she waved her hands at the shelves. "Oh, you know…options, right? Very exciting. Do you want pre-sifted? Unbleached?"

Paul wrinkled his brow, but the rest of his expression remained carefully neutral. "Any of these would be fine. Whatever's cheapest, I think."

Karen grabbed a bag of all-purpose flour, and strode away, swiping baking powder and a bag of chocolate chips as well. She dumped the supplies on the conveyor belt at the first checkout, then headed for the dairy section. "Need eggs?" She tossed the question over her shoulder, but didn't wait for a response. She needed a minute to compose herself. This reaction was bizarre. She'd only had one conversation with the man. Sure, she'd observed him in a creepy stalker fashion for weeks, but they barely knew each other. She'd gotten carried away with some romantic fantasy of the good-looking cop next door.

"Megan says we need milk." Paul stepped up beside her. Karen looked around. "She got sucked into your magazine display."

"Oh."

"For dunking."

"I'm sorry?"

"The milk. We'll need it once the cookies are cool." He grinned. "Or so I've been instructed."

Good lord, that smile could light up a room.

"It's a classic combination," she breathed, kicking herself as the words came out sounding funny. He must have heard the warble too, because his gaze dropped to her mouth and lingered for a moment. "What kind do you want?"

He flicked his gaze back to her eyes and blinked. "1%, I guess."

"It's behind the last door there."

He brushed past, close enough for her skin to prickle, but not quite making physical contact, and she sucked in a breath. He paused, because how could he not have heard it, but then he opened the cooler and pulled out a bag of milk.

They stood for a minute, her with the eggs, him with the milk, and he smiled again, but this time it seemed wistful. "You're an interesting neighbour to have, Karen."

"Thanks, I guess." Her lips curled up of their own volition. "You're unlike any neighbour I've ever had."

"I came to Wardham for peace and quiet, you know."

She couldn't contain her surprise. "You think I'm a troublemaker?"

He grinned. "I'm quite certain you are."

"And you don't like trouble." It spilled out before she could filter the words into something less pleading. "I mean—"

"I have a professional interest in avoiding it." He interrupted her, but his tone wasn't rude. It was warm and low and full of...*heat*? He stepped closer. "On a personal level, I have a history of liking trouble more than I should."

Oh, shit. "I've never been trouble before," she whispered.

His knuckles brushed hers. Milk, eggs and a boatload of issues apparently stood between them, but at that moment, all she could feel were the hard, hot points of contact as the back of his hand pressed into her skin. His words, when they came, drifted toward her as if through a fog. "This is probably too much."

"Yeah." She took a big step back and shook her head. "You're right. I'm sorry."

"You don't need to be sorry." He laughed. "They're our groceries. I'm not sure we need eggs."

Oh. So she'd invented a whole moment there. Fantastic. "You'll use them up. Hard boil them for lunches."

She spun on her heel to head for the checkout again, but he reached out and stilled her movement with a press of his hand to her arm. "Karen..."

"Mmmm?"

"Thank you."

"No problem." She shot him a bright smile. "Just being neighbourly."

He nodded, then took a breath and held it, as if he had been about to say something, but changed his mind.

Her imagination could do wonderful things with that pause, but Karen didn't harbour any illusions. Paul wouldn't be the first crush she'd gotten over. Probably not the last. "Really, it's fine. Come on, let's find Megan. You guys have cookies to bake."

She nodded her head down the aisle, but his hand still lingered. Warmth transferred through her shirt and sent tendrils of want slithering throughout her body. What would it be like to have him touch her bare arm? Her neck? Her breasts? Not here, of course. It would have to be somewhere private. Maybe on a weeknight he didn't have Megan...

"Dad? You get everything?" *Megan*! Crap on a stick.

Karen took a giant step back, bumping into the endcap. She whirled and headed for the cash. What was she thinking? Maybe she was more trouble than she thought.

The idea gave her more pleasure than it should.

3

———

KAREN copied the last files to the online dropbox for her bookkeeper and stretched back in her chair. Managing a grocery store required a surprising amount of butt-in-chair time. It was one of the reasons she walked or biked to work, even in the winter. That was pretty much the only exercise she got.

"Hey, boss, you wanted me to remind you to get the hell out at 3:30."

She glanced toward the door of her office with a rueful smile. "I'm pretty sure I didn't mean for you to repeat my awful language, Mitchell Wagner."

The high school senior flashed a grin that they both knew was effectively disarming.

"Where did you learn to be so charming? I remember it wasn't so long ago that you were cracking butt jokes."

"Chicks don't like crudeness."

"We don't like to be called chicks, either."

Another grin.

"Whatever, my weekend is finally here, I don't care." She glanced at the schedule on the wall. "I'll see you Tuesday." She pushed away from the desk and headed to the front of the store.

Her favourite part-time cashier, Melody, was waiting with an overflowing shopping bag. "Here, I packed you some food because I noticed you didn't eat lunch."

"Am I going to have to cook it?"

Melody laughed. "I gave you both options. There's pita, hummus, lettuce, tomatoes and falafels, already cooked, but I also gave you a big-ass steak and some mushrooms. It's a nice day to grill."

"Grilling I can handle. Thanks, sweetie."

And that was why the last decade had passed in a blur. For all that she never saw herself taking over from her parents, running the store meant that she spent every day with awesome people, both staff and customers, in the heart of the town she loved. And at the end of the day, she got to stroll home, and sit on her deck with a cold beer and a good book.

When she reflected on it like that, she felt guilty for complaining. And yet...it wasn't her passion. It was good, but it wasn't great.

Too bad she didn't have the drive to go for great. Good would have to be enough.

As if the universe had signaled to her mother that her oldest child was considering traitorous revolt, Karen's phone rang out with the dedicated Beyonce ring tone Grace Miller hated. She shifted the bag of groceries to her other hip and dug it out. "What beautiful part of the warm south are you and Dad in this week?"

Her mother laughed gently at the other end of the phone. "We arrived in Phoenix last night. Staying at the same camp we visited last year. Your brother's got a couple of days off after the games this weekend. Do you want to fly down?"

"Mom..." Karen hated this conversation. Her parents offered on a regular basis, and her younger siblings took them up on it, but she didn't like to take advantage. Maybe it was because she knew the ins and outs of their business, and how much the store made. Her parents were comfortable, but not independently wealthy by any stretch of the imagination. Chase did well, and he was generous, which Karen was also uncomfortable with, but these offers were coming out their pocket, not his. "I see Chase when he plays Detroit. And when he's home in the summer. Plus I need to work."

"You should hire a part-time manager."

"Actually...I wanted to talk to you about that."

"Hiring someone? Go for it."

"Not exactly." Karen had practiced this conversation many times over the last couple years. It hadn't helped.

"Is this about the community centre?"

"So you heard."

"I can't believe it took you two weeks to tell me."

"Mom..." The truth was, she wasn't sure what she wanted to say.

"I know, Kare-Bear."

"Okay, I'm thirty-four. The nickname can be retired."

"Never. You're my first baby, you're stuck with it. So, what are you thinking? Do you want to go back to school?"

Karen trudged up her driveway. The front door was locked, but the back wasn't, and if she went in off the deck, she wouldn't need to dig for keys. "That didn't work out so well the first time."

"That was ten years ago."

"I'd have to sell my house." She mentally ran through the list of universities that offered library science programs. It was probably telling that she didn't have to think very hard to summon the information.

"You could rent it out."

And pay rent in London or Toronto? And tuition? She knew the offer that would come next and she'd nip it in the bud. "Whatever I decide to do, Mom, I'll be doing it myself."

"You're too stubborn."

"And you're too generous." She pushed into her kitchen and dumped the bag of groceries on the counter before heading back to the deck to start the barbeque. "Listen, I just got home, and I haven't had lunch yet. Can I talk to you later?"

"Of course. Hey, remember to call your sister!" The baby of the family, Audrey was studying at the University of Windsor just down the road. But for as often as they saw each other, it might as well have been a plane ride away. Thirteen years separated them, and Karen sometimes worried that might be an insurmountable barrier to real friendship like her friend Evie had with her sister, Laney. "Karen?"

"Yep, I'll call her. How are her exams going?" *See, Mom? I know what's going on.*

"Oh, fine, I think. You remember what twenty-one was like. She's not big on sharing with me right now." Grace laughed. "Seems that doesn't really change. Remember, honey, your dad and I don't need to travel this much. If you want to just take a leave of absence from the store, we'll come home, no questions asked."

It sounded like the perfect solution. So why didn't it ease the tug of worry in her stomach?

She mulled over the options while she munched on a torn piece of pita and put away the rest of her groceries. Thoughts crashed together in her brain as she grabbed a beer and the steak and headed outside. By the time she'd flipped it over for the last few minutes of grilling, she was no closer to clarity, and she had a pounding headache to boot.

"Hi, Karen!" Megan's high, clear voice rang out behind her. Karen turned and smiled as the girl crossed the asphalt drive between their decks and climbed up Karen's stairs.

"Hey to you, too." Karen looked around, but Paul was nowhere to be seen. "Where's your dad?"

"On the phone with my mom. I'm hiding."

"Oh."

"It's okay. He's just asking her if I can be a bit late going home tomorrow, he wants to take me to a football game."

"Fun." Megan raised one eyebrow and Karen couldn't help but laugh. "Not fun?"

"He makes it fun, but I'd rather just hang out here and read or something."

"You should tell him that." The words were out of her mouth before she could stop them. "I mean, you could tell him that. He'd probably like to know that you're happy spending time with him wherever."

"Yeah..."

Karen turned back to her barbeque for a moment to pull the steak off onto the waiting plate. She turned the propane off and set the meat aside to rest before moving to the steps of her deck and taking a seat. She patted the wood beside her. "Sit, tell me what you're reading right now while you wait for your dad."

———

TALKING to Susan always set Paul on edge. It wasn't like his ex said anything explicit, but he could always hear an undercurrent of judgment and concern in her voice. As if he needed reminding that sleep was important on a school night. The game would be over by 6:30, so even with traffic, Megan would be home well before eight. And the needling about not trying too hard...*God.* Of course he needed to try hard.

Through the back window he could see Megan sitting on Karen's deck, her knees pulled up under chin as she listened to Karen talk about something big and exciting, judging by her hand gestures and animated facial expressions. His daughter laughed, and the tension in his chest eased. Moving to Wardham had been a good decision. It was Saturday afternoon and he wasn't going to be paged, didn't need to have a babysitter on standby, wouldn't catch flack from Susan for neglecting his time with Megan again. He had a backyard for the first time in six years.

He shook off his melancholy mood. It was time to take advantage of the warm spring day.

He grabbed a pack of burgers from the freezer and stuck his head outside. "Meg, burgers okay for dinner?"

She nodded, and reluctantly stood up.

"Stay." He glanced at Karen, taking a moment to appreciate her warm beauty. That was okay. It was inevitable, so it had to be okay. "It'll take me a few minutes to get things ready, keep talking. If it's okay with Karen, I mean."

"Of course." Her smile carried all the way to her eyes, and she held his gaze for an extra second before turning back to Megan and resuming what sounded like a discussion about book length.

The barbeque on his deck was ancient. It had come with the house, but he'd used it twice already. He cranked the propane and reached for the lighter, knowing that the igniter switch didn't work. It took a few tries, but eventually both burners caught and he lowered the lid to build up the heat.

Back inside, he assembled buns, condiments and vegetables on a tray to carry outside. It was warm enough to eat an early dinner on the deck. He perused the contents of his fridge, which still hadn't reached that happy full stage, and decided on beer for himself and lemonade for Megan.

When he returned to the deck, the conversation had wandered in a different direction. *Cute guys? No way is Megan old enough for that.* He gave them a minute while he got the burgers going, and then interjected. "Hey now, Dad alert—want to not give me a heart attack, here?'

Megan and Karen ducked their heads together and giggled. His daughter raised her eyebrows and taunted him a sing-song voice. "Would you rather we talk about cute girls?"

He had enough self-control to not flick his gaze toward Karen, but out of the corner of his eye he saw her blush, and that was enough to send his mind spiraling into the gutter. He cleared his throat and willed his cock not to respond. It ignored him completely. *How far down her chest does that blush spread? What else makes her turn so deliciously pink?*

He tried to distract himself by setting the table, but his baser-self jeered at him the whole time. As a man, he couldn't help but notice women. *Particularly this woman.* In fact, since he'd met Karen, he really hadn't noticed anyone else. And more often than not, he was being visited in his dreams by a brunette with a big smile and bouncy breasts.

Not that he was blaming his sub-conscious. He couldn't do that, when he let his waking thoughts drift to her as well. Just that morning he'd taken himself to the brink in the shower, imagining—

"Dad!" Megan's shriek pulled him out of his thoughts, and her wild gestures in the direction of his barbeque, flames licking out along the edge of the lid, black smoke pluming into the air.

"Oh for fuck's sake," he muttered, leaping forward to flip the lid up, then ducking beneath the unit to turn off the propane. As the flames sputtered out beneath the charred remains of their still smoking burgers, he had to give a nod to the universe for reminding him where his focus needed to be—and where it couldn't be.

Behind him, the deck creaked, and he glanced back at Karen and Megan who were approaching the barbeque with horrified expressions.

"I'm not eating that," Meg said resolutely, crossing her arms.

Paul sighed. "Of course not."

"Carbon gives you cancer."

"I think I've got a frozen pizza I can pull out." He raised his eyebrows at his daughter's sullen expression. "You have an interesting ability to go from happy to mad in no time flat, kiddo."

She scowled, but he wanted to believe he also saw chagrin melt into her expression.

"Uhm," Karen glanced between them cautiously. "I have a giant steak over there, already grilled. I could slice it up, and we could use your buns to make steak sandwiches?"

Meg perked up at the suggestion, and Paul couldn't think of a good reason to beg off and not incur the wrath of a ten-year-old for being stubborn and "weird". He didn't really understand what that meant, but to Meg, it was the highest order of insults.

He nodded. "That would be awesome, thank you, Karen."

She blushed again, and he wondered at the contradiction. For someone so personable, she didn't seem comfortable with much attention. *Or maybe she's picking up on the fact that your attention isn't just friendly.* He cursed himself for possibly making her uncomfortable. Playing at straight and upstanding would take more effort than he'd put into it so far. *Or you could try actually being a good neighbour instead of fantasizing inappropriately about her at every turn.* He shook his head. Now his subconscious was lecturing him like they were separate people. Probably something that a psychologist would love to delve into. Him, not so much, and yet there it was on his mind.

Before he could think about that much further, she'd gone and returned, bearing not just a drool-worthy steak, but also veggies and hummus, and a drink for herself. He gestured for her to pull up a chair, resisting the excuse to get closer and pull it out for her.

After they'd stuffed themselves, Paul handed over the phone and urged Megan to call her mother to say goodnight. She rolled her eyes, but skipped inside quickly enough he knew it was the right suggestion. He felt compelled to fill the sudden silence of the backyard with an explanation. "She hates it when Susan and I fight, even about something little." He shifted in his seat. "Her mother is better at reassuring—"

"It's okay, you don't need to explain." Her voice was soft and low, and her expression was without guile. "I mean, if you want to talk about it, I'm happy to listen, but from the little I've seen, it seems like you're handling it as well as anyone would."

HE LET OUT A SHORT, humourless laugh. That would be a quick way to end any possibility of Karen being attracted to him. Let her see just how badly he'd handled being a dad.

If his bark raised any questions, they didn't show in her eyes. Her gaze held his just long enough to remind him of her offer to listen, then drifted to the back of the yard when it became clear he wasn't going to take her offer. But maybe he could return it.

"How about you?"

"What about me?" She wrinkled her brow in honest confusion.

A dozen questions slammed into his head. He wanted to know why she was cooking a steak for one. Why she was surprised at the chemistry between them. Where her support network was, and how she managed to get his daughter to talk about things without scowling. What her favourite books were and if she liked movies. Popcorn or candy at the theatre. Her favourite season. Colour of her sheets. Her bra.

"Paul?"

He cleared his throat. "You talked to Meg about books, you would listen to me piss and moan...isn't it your turn to unload?"

She cocked an eyebrow. "You offering?"

Had no one done that before? "Yeah. I'm offering."

"You don't even know me."

"I know you as well as you know me." Something flickered in her eyes, a flare of worry. If he didn't have a decade of experience interviewing people with something to hide, he'd probably have missed it. "Unless you think you know me better..."

Bingo. She flushed, this time not so delicately. Her lower lip sucked in between her teeth, and her eyes widened. An honest, innocent response that made him feel two feet tall for poking at her.

He leaned forward in his chair and braced his forearms against his thighs, hands splayed in an open gesture. "Hey, whatever it is, I'm sure it's not as bad as you think." He offered what he hoped came across as a gentle smile. "Did you go through my garbage? Email me from a fake account? Spy on me with binoculars?"

She returned his smile, although hers was more tenuous and her brow remained furrowed. "It's just that you're somewhat a hot topic of conversation, and in Wardham, those types of conversations tend to happen at the grocery store."

"So you've been gossiping about me?" He let out a hoot and settled back in his chair. The idea of Karen lapping up bits of information about him over the checkout belt warmed him from the inside out. "First of all, darlin', that doesn't mean you know me. And second, it's not something to get all flustered over. You need to brass these things out. Or don't gossip in the first place if it makes you feel so bad."

She narrowed her eyes and crossed her arms across her chest, plumping up her breasts. Not the right moment to get distracted. She was going to scold him, and then brush it off, just like she had the first time they met. He could see it coming and had to restrain himself from grinning in broad delight.

"You're…"

"Yeah?"

"I don't know. But I don't feel bad about gossiping about you now." She scowled, but the heat was already fading.

"Good. Now tell me what has you out of sorts."

"I'm not—" Except she was, and recognition that he had her number flashed across her face. "How did you know that I was out of sorts?"

"You stomped up the drive earlier, and you've had a distracted look on your face ever since."

"I didn't stomp."

"It was cute."

"Shut up." She sighed and closed her eyes. "I was talking to my mom."

He waited. It didn't take long.

"I haven't always worked at the grocery store. I mean, I have, really. I started bagging groceries when I was twelve, and before that I helped stock shelves on Sundays. But I took a break when I went to university." The words poured out like maple syrup. Smooth and shiny, fast and sweet. She'd given this spiel before.

"And when my parents decided to retire, I'd just moved home. So it made sense to take over managing the store."

"Your idea?"

"I don't remember." After pausing for a sip of beer, she shook her head. Her next words didn't come out smoothly, or quickly. "It was their idea. It benefited them as much as me, but…"

"You think they did it for you."

She managed to nod and shake her head at the same time, which made him laugh. "It was a good thing. Really. For all of us. They got to travel more freely, without selling the store, and I had a job at a time when I needed one. And when they came home for the summer, I could take as much time off as I wanted."

"So what's changed?"

"Nothing. And that's the problem. A decade has flitted by in the blink of an eye, and I still don't know what I want to do when I grow up. And I'm in my thirties, so I can't pretend that an awesome life is still going to happen." She grimaced and looked down at her beer bottle. While they'd been talking, she'd worried the label with her thumbnail, and now she peeled the whole thing off.

Paul felt his cock flex against the denim of his jeans. He had a flashback to high school, and a teasing game from the first drinking parties he attended. Sometimes a fully intact peeled label meant one was sexually frustrated. Other times it meant you would get lucky. It depended on which dominant teen queen was making up the rules that night. He'd never wanted the latter to be as true as he did in that moment, and never before had the former been more guaranteed.

He needed to change the subject. "You want another beer? I should check on Megan, too." She nodded as he stood up.

When he returned, she'd moved to stand at the back of his deck, leaning against the rail.

"Meg's done talking to her mom, but now she's catching up on a reality show she recorded. I should go in and watch it with her, but watching people embarrass themselves..." He mock shuddered. "And it's two hours long! Who has time for that?"

"Hey, I love shows like that!"

"Do you want to go in there and supervise for me, then?" He rested his elbows on the railing next to her. They weren't close enough to touch, not quite, but he could still feel her. It was almost as good as the real thing. *Not even close.*

She pulled back and cocked head to look at him. "Feel free to tell me to mind my own p's and q's, but why do you need to watch it with her?"

"I don't know." He meant that in every way. He had no clue what was appropriate parenting for a ten-year-old. He didn't know why he couldn't relax about the new custody arrangement.

He definitely couldn't remember why he'd banned himself from dating.

"Susan—my ex-wife—called me on not pulling my weight a couple of years ago. It's been a rocky path back to what we have now. With both of them. And it still feels like I'm in precarious waters." It was more than he'd shared with anyone, and he shocked himself even as he opened up further. "There's only so much selfish that one is allowed in a lifetime, and I've used up my allotment."

Her gaze was steady and pressing. He could feel it even though he still stared straight ahead. She let the silence hang until he filled it, a trick he used all the time and didn't expect to fall for, but she had him off-kilter. She had him wanting to explain. To justify.

"I'm no martyr. I *want* to focus on being a dad for the next while. Get that right, you know? Besides, you're one to talk. No awesome life in front of you? What's that bull?"

She shrugged. "I shouldn't have said that. My life is good."

"What would make it better?"

"I dunno. Adventure, maybe?" She straightened to a stand and set her beer on the railing. "Maybe I need to be a little selfish. I haven't used up anywhere near my allotment."

Physical pain sliced through his chest at the image of Karen getting her wild on while he embraced responsibility. If only they'd met at another time, in another place. He'd have shot for the moon and the stars with her, and made the trip just as interesting as the destination. But that wasn't an option here and now, as he started over. He was grounded in this place where she was stifled, a place he'd spent almost two years wiggling his way towards. They were two ships passing in the night. That slap of reality hurt more than he could have imagined.

4

———

A WEEK had gone by and she'd seen Paul almost every day. They hadn't talked, touched or otherwise interacted, but his presence surrounded her. Even if the detachment building wasn't one block from the store, and their paths likely to cross as they just went about their daily business, he was right next door each evening.

That made for long nights. Their conversation played over again and again in her head. The physical memory of his body next to hers, just standing chastely on his deck, fueled more than a few fantasies. Where instead of gruffly bidding her a good evening and escaping inside to watch TV with his daughter, Paul had closed the gap between them and proposed an entirely different and deliciously inappropriate adventure for them to embark on together.

Karen had never been titillated by dirty words until Hot Neighbour, the fantasy version of Paul that only existed in her head, had urged her to spread her legs and show him how wet she was for him. There was nothing imaginary about the answer, and if she hadn't been alone in her bedroom, she might have been embarrassed at how her body reacted to someone who was so obviously off limits to her.

But there was a line between harmless fantasy and unrequited desire, and she wasn't going to end up on the pathetic side of the division. By Thursday, she'd had enough of wanting what she couldn't have. Ironically, it was Paul's own words that spurred her to action. She definitely couldn't have him, but she could have an adventure of another sort. After a few nights of internet research, she knew what she needed to do, and who she needed to talk to.

Leaving Wardham would have given her pause a month ago, but it was time to find her own brand of selfish. She'd have liked to find it with the guy next door, but he'd done all but announce he was off-limits and not interested. So the new plan meant she needed to stop wanting to get naked with Paul.

The plan would be easier to implement if he didn't live next door. If Wardham wasn't so small. If, if, if.

The Sunday night book club crew hadn't helped with the distraction, either. The discussion had wandered off topic more than once in the direction of the new cop, and Ernie Fletcher took one of those opportunities to share with the group that Karen had let her neighbour and his daughter do after hours shopping. The group was divided on whether or not that was appropriate, which normally would have flowed around and past Karen as normal Wardham meddling, but last night she'd snapped and before she realized what she was sharing, she promised Ernie and the other busy bodies that pretty soon, she wouldn't have keys to the grocery store anyway.

So it was with extreme reluctance that she headed to Main Street on Monday morning. She had an appointment she wanted to keep, and she wanted coffee and a muffin first. She'd hedged her bets and waited until 8:15 before stepping into the bakery/coffee shop. Ten minutes after school drop off, fifteen minutes before the medical building and most businesses opened. A guaranteed line, and no privacy for Carrie to take advantage of to start a heavy conversation. Perfect.

Karen wasn't in the mood to talk. She was unsettled. Had been for a few weeks. Since meeting Paul, in fact, but it wasn't him. It was the library, and her parents, and last night's brouhaha. But she wasn't so confident in her still tenuous plan that she could justify it to her best friend—because she couldn't trust Carrie to be supportive.

Surely it should be her choice if she didn't want to manage the grocery store. And as the daughter of the owners, she could make a suggestion as to how to proceed with dealing with the loss of their manager. They could hire someone else, sure, but why not consider selling to a national chain? Her parents didn't need income any more. And the proceeds from the sale would help pad their nest egg a bit anyway.

Everyone just needed to mind their own business.

Because she could sense the meddling approaching. She didn't know what form it would take, but it was close. Carrie was the obvious person to address the common concern about the store's fate. And she would, because their friendship could handle it, and she wouldn't want Karen to be blindsided by anyone else.

So Karen knew it was coming. But she also wanted a coffee and a muffin. Tough choice.

This weighed heavy on her mind as she stood in line. She wasn't counting on the next person to step into the shop behind her to be wearing a uniform.

Oh god. In running gear, he was hot. In jeans and a hoodie, he was cute.

His pressed, dark blue uniform, complete with a Kevlar vest with POLICE printed on it, turned his lean length into something approaching a superhero's physique. Tall, broad across the shoulders, narrow at the hips. The newfound troublemaker in her wanted to know where on his black utility belt his handcuffs were, but there was only so much staring at his waist that she could do without being weird. Besides, she needed to keep looking at the rest of him. Up and down, and all around. There was a lot to take in.

In his uniform, Paul was out of this world. Hot and cute didn't begin to describe the pure masculinity that rolled off him. His expression was carefully neutral, but he'd blinked twice when he saw her and that was enough.

She affected him.

It should have felt like vindication, but it didn't. Instead, the realization left her sad. Hollow. Because it didn't matter.

She pasted on a polite smile and murmured a generic greeting.

He nodded, but didn't say anything. The line shuffled forward and she turned her back to him, pretending to examine the display of baked goods. Another reason to be grateful. If Carrie wasn't swamped at the counter, she'd have called foul on that action alone. Karen knew the complete line up of Bun's offerings inside and out. There was no need to peer at the muffins like she didn't know that the top row was Morning Glory, Raisin Bran and Oatmeal Banana, or the "breakfast offerings" as Carrie branded them.

His voice, when he used it, was low and right behind her. "What's good?"

She twisted enough to not be rude, but not so far that they'd share eye contact. Eye contact was not in the plan.

"Everything," she whispered. "But you should get the raisin bran."

"Why?"

"Low fat."

"You think I need to watch what I eat?" She could hear the smile in his voice and immediately regretted the plan. She really wanted to turn around. See that she amused him. Raise an eyebrow and point out without saying a word that she *knew* him. Let him wipe away her annoyance with a smirk and a wink.

She settled for reminding him that she had his number. "I think *you* think you do."

The bell chimed, and two more people joined the curving line. She shifted forward, but he moved more, and then he was in her personal space. And she could smell him.

Sport body wash and something else. Laundry soap, maybe. She took a deep breath in, trying to be surreptitious.

"Maybe I need to step outside my comfort zone."

She swallowed hard. Yeah, maybe he did, but he wouldn't. With muffins, or her, or anything else. She should have seen that coming. From his car to making his daughter put oatmeal in her chocolate chip cookies, Paul was clearly comfortable with the safe choices in life. Maybe that was from his job, or maybe something else in his past, but right now, his comfort zone was exactly where he needed to be. "Risk is overrated. Have the raisin bran muffin. It's good."

She was the next person in line, and she could see that Carrie already had her latte in a takeaway cup. She dug exact change out of her pocket and stepped to the counter. "I'll take a Morning Glory muffin," she said to the cashier. "And can you toss a knife and a pat of butter in the bag?"

Without looking over her shoulder, she grabbed her breakfast and headed for the door. She was almost home free when she heard Paul say, "I'll have the same thing. Two pats of butter, please."

Her stomach pitched in an unexpected but not unpleasant way, and she mulled over how much she could read into a muffin purchase all the way to the library. It wasn't until Mildred waved her into the back office that Karen realized that strange interaction with Paul had completely distracted her from her concerns about the store and what people might be thinking.

The librarian followed her into the room and closed the door.

Karen dug into her muffin, buying herself a few moments to rearrange her thoughts.

"Thanks for meeting me here." She swallowed a last bite and brushed a napkin across her lips. "I appreciate the privacy."

"I heard that you want to quit at the store."

"That was quick."

"It's Wardham." Mildred shrugged. "And if it wasn't your parents' store, this would have happened a long time ago."

Karen sighed. "I'd like to think that, but honestly, I'm not sure. It still feels scary to say that I want to move on to something else without knowing what that might be."

"I think I have an idea."

"Okay, so I have some idea." Karen laughed. "I guess it's asking too much for me to blink and wake up with the degree? Why can't I just be a librarian without going back to school?"

The older woman shot her a rueful smile. "Times have changed. I feel your pain, sweetie. I wouldn't have this job if I'd have had to get a Masters' degree first."

"What if I fail again?"

"Can I be blunt?"

"Have you ever not been?"

"You didn't fail the first time." Mildred lifted her hand to halt the protest. "You didn't. You quit. That's not the same thing as not being able to complete the program with the right motivation."

"I was motivated. I wanted to be a librarian."

"You wanted to get people to read books." Mildred didn't need to finish that thought. They both knew that being a librarian was about more than that, and Karen hadn't loved the rest of it. They both knew that the day she'd decided to stay in Wardham and not head back to school after the Christmas break was a happy day. For her. For her parents, who'd been quick to suggest they could head down to Florida to watch Chase play hockey.

Ten years later, and she was finally ready to move on to something else.

"So what can I do? What options are there for a read-a-holic who hates school?"

"Honestly, I don't know, but I'll look into it and let you know. In larger centres, there's more diversity in the jobs posted. And I'd be happy to be a reference for you."

Moving for a job. She hadn't considered that variation on the plan. Of course she'd have to move. She knew all of the jobs in Wardham. Knew she wasn't qualified for half of them, and wasn't interested in the other half. But she'd been thinking about leaving for a year, going back to school. Her heart sank, but her head stayed in the game.

"Thank you, I appreciate that. Any information you can share...I told my mom that I wanted to be done mid-summer. I want to take a road trip out west before starting...whatever I do next. But for the right job, I could be available any time."

Mildred nodded and stood up. "You heading to the store now? Or do you want to hang out here for a bit?"

A wave of relief washed over Karen. She pulled out her e-reader and grinned. "I'm going to hide here, if you don't mind." She'd have to go to the store later, but it could wait until the next rush at Bun. She didn't need to give Carrie an obvious opening. Her friend would find her soon enough.

5

———

DOWNTOWN Wardham had been a pleasant surprise for Paul. The main drag was only a few blocks long, but it had one of almost every essential service. Karen's grocery store, Bun, a dry cleaner's, pharmacy, even a couple of clothing stores and a used bookshop.

And then there was his destination for the evening, Danny's. Paul had heard good things about the pub. Cold beer, cheap wings, and like everything else in Wardham, it was only a few blocks from home. Stumbling distance, not that he was going to get blitzed. But it'd been a long week at work, and a short weekend with Megan.

Night. Not a weekend. Susan had smoothly talked him into taking his daughter back to the city that afternoon instead of the next day, as per their custody agreement. Her family had an annual picnic and she had pressed home the point that Meg didn't have any family on his side. As if that was somehow in his domain of control.

Whose fault is it that you're an island of one?

A question he'd been asked by Susan, the department psychiatrist, and, when he was being honest, himself more than once.

He never had an answer, and tonight wasn't any different.

Tonight he just wanted to kick back and relax. Maybe be a bit social. *Just a bit.* It was all he had in him.

The pub was long, narrow and surprisingly busy given how few cars had been parked outside. As a law enforcement officer, he was grateful for that fact. He'd been on the scene of too many devastating accidents caused by impaired drivers.

"Paul!"

He turned, half expecting the greeting to be directed at someone else—but really, how many people in Wardham knew his name? The obvious answer thudded into his brain at the same moment he found her face in the crowd. Karen stepped closer, dragging a smaller blond woman behind her.

"Hey, neighbour," she breathed, then flashed a wide smile. He felt the words as if she'd pressed close and whispered them against his skin, but her expression was straight up friendly, no undercurrent of sexual tension. If anything, she seemed eager to put her friend between them. She pushed the petite blond forward another step. "This is Evie. She's got two kids a bit younger than Megan."

Evie grimaced at him, then laughed. "And therefore we are going to be the best of friends. Single parents unite."

"We can do the secret handshake when she's not looking," he said, and chuckled.

"I didn't mean it like that! Jeez. Give a girl a break, eh?" Karen blushed and again Paul would swear he could actually feel her flush warm against his own skin. Shared visceral reactions, that was a damn neat trick. He stepped back and shook it off.

Evie gave him a quizzical look, then invited him to join them at their table. "No pressure, but I don't think you're going to find a table all to yourself right now."

"Yeah, I see that. Is it usually this busy?"

She shook her head. "Wing special tonight. It'll empty out in an hour. People have evening chores."

Two hours later, the pub had indeed emptied out. Karen had made sure he'd been introduced to half the patrons, which he could have done without, and he'd thought about heading out a half dozen times. He'd made it as far as the door once, but a tall blond man who looked like he spent most of his days tossing hay bales and herding cattle had chosen that moment to wrap his arms around Karen from behind and nuzzle his face into her neck. Something ugly and mean twisted in Paul's gut and he'd drifted back toward the bar. She'd pushed the muscle bound farmer off with a playful grin, but her personal space kept getting invaded. He signaled for another beer after deciding to wait until he could walk her home.

He had absolutely no right to care about who she socialized with. But he did care, a lot. And the gentle way she flirted, with kindness and without promise, brought their private encounters into sharp contrast. This wasn't his Karen. This woman was lovely to everyone who approached her, but there was no sexual innuendo, no game.

She'd made a brief conversation about muffins mean something important, she'd given him that, and he couldn't walk away from her tonight.

When he'd gotten back to work that morning, he'd eyed the brown paper bag, shiny with grease spots, and wondered what exactly was in a Morning Glory muffin. It had, in fact, tasted amazing, but in an "extra-long run required to make this worthwhile" kind of way.

She'd told him to get a raisin bran muffin. She was right. That would have been his choice. Maybe should have been. But he'd gotten the distinct impression that she wasn't just talking about a muffin, and he didn't want her to think for a second that she wasn't wanted.

Yeah, she was wanted.

Her hair had been up in some sort of thick, twisty bun that morning. He'd stood behind her trying to figure out how many bobby pins he'd have to pull out before her curls tumbled loose. The thought of her hair spilling into his hands, over her shoulders, maybe over *his* shoulders if he was close enough...had made him instantly hard.

And just like that, the memory had the same effect on him again in Danny's. Watching her have fun. With other men, who meant nothing, but were free to fill the space around her.

Fuck. He wanted to be free to tuck her close to him, sit wide on the barstool and tug her between his thighs. Pull her back against his chest and declare to all comers that she was taken. And he was pretty sure she'd let him.

Because Karen wasn't playing a game. Games, maybe, for fun, but when it came to a relationship, she'd be straight up. Why hadn't he found her sooner? Before he was bitter and broken?

"Hey, is this stool taken?" He glanced up from his beer. The redhead from work.

"Carrie, hi. Sure, have a seat."

"Uhm." She shifted in place, biting her lip. "It's Stella, actually."

"Shit, really? Sorry."

"It's okay."

"No, it's not. How long have I been calling you Carrie?"

She let out a watery laugh. "Like, a month."

"I'm an idiot."

"You were probably thinking of my cousin's wife, Carrie Nixon. Well, she's a Nixon by marriage, but still, it's close."

"Is she the one at the coffee shop?"

She nodded.

"Right. Well, I've been calling her Stella."

She laughed again, this time with more confidence. The bartender heard her and skipped over with a raised eyebrow. "Hey, Stel. Usual?"

"Yep, thanks, Mari."

He waited until the brunette behind the bar drifted away before broaching the subject. "Uhm, Stella...should she have carded you?"

Another laugh, this one dissolving into a giggle. "No. We went to high school together. She knows I'm twenty two."

"I'm sorry, it's just that I might not have remembered your name, but I know that you're in your first year of college."

She shifted again, a faint flush colouring her cheeks. "It took me a while to get there."

"Nothing wrong with that."

She nodded, and he was glad he hadn't asked more. They sat together in companionable silence for a moment, picking through the pretzel bowl.

"How are you liking Wardham so far?"

He shrugged. "Everyone seems nice. Pretty town, not a lot of a crime."

"Is that good, or boring?"

"Boring is good. I've had enough of hunting bad guys every day."

She smiled at that, and he couldn't help but return the grin. Even if he hadn't remembered her name, this girl was a prime example of just how nice the people of Wardham could be. That made him think of the nicest member of the Chamber of Commerce, and he spun on his stool to look for Karen. He found her quickly. Too quickly. She was leaning against the back wall, being talked at by the blond farmer, but her gaze was firmly pinned on Paul, and she didn't look pleased.

He wrinkled his brow, asking the obvious question. Her sweeping look at Stella, then back to him, made the disapproval obvious. He chuckled. Oh, she was too cute. The warmth of a few beers had eased his usual tight rein, and after watching her flirt all night, he was done with being restrained.

"I'm heading out." He left his beer bottle on the bar and tapped the intern on her shoulder. "See you next week."

He took his time standing up, enjoying the play of emotions dance across Karen's face. Without breaking eye contact, he strolled across the pub. When he reached her, he stretched his hand out to the farmer with a terse introduction, but kept his attention focused on his neighbour. His beautiful, jealous neighbour.

————

"I THOUGHT I'd head home, wanted to see if you'd like some company for the walk." His voice was low, meant for her ears only, and the rich timbre rubbed into her heart like a soothing balm.

A balm she'd do her best to resist. What on earth was he thinking, chatting up a woman a dozen years his junior? When he'd made it crystal clear that he wasn't interested in dating.

Unless that was a lie, and it was just *her* he didn't want to date. The thought slipped out of her mind and wrapped itself around her throat. He wouldn't do that. Would he? She really didn't know him. Frankly, she was pretty sure she knew his daughter better. Megan wouldn't deceive someone to spare their feelings. God love ten-year-olds and their straightforward approach to life.

"You're doing that thing again, thinking on your face." He ducked his head, bringing his lips to her ears. "I'd love to see what that looks like when you're turned on."

She jerked away, bumping into the wall behind her. "You're drunk."

"Little bit. Will you be my safety walk home?" He glanced to the man at her left. She'd dated Blake for five minutes a decade earlier, before he moved on to Portia Wilkins. He was still fun to hang out with at Danny's, but there was zero chemistry. In both directions, which was the story of her life. Paul didn't need to know that, though.

"I don't know if I can, we were just..." Crap on a stick. She couldn't play that game. "You know what? Yes. I'd like to walk home with you."

Blake headed to a table at the back with a shrug and she grabbed her sweater.

They were almost to the end of the main drag before either of them spoke. The silence was nice, and Karen wasn't sure how much talking she wanted a tipsy Paul to do. On the one hand, she really wanted him to whisper more in her ear about sex. On the other, he would regret it in the morning, and go back to pretending he liked being celibate.

"You don't have anything to be jealous about," he said, as they turned the corner to their street. The entire town was quiet. It wasn't late, probably only nine o'clock, but there was enough of a nip in the air that anyone who could be was inside, curled up on a couch.

"I wasn't—"

"—yeah, you were. Your face, remember?" She would have argued again, but the words stilled on the tip of her tongue as he slipped his hand around hers. Good lord, holding hands with him made her twitchy with want.

"Stella's quite young. And you work with her."

"I know. And I know. I wasn't flirting with her, I promise. She's one of the few people I know here, that's all."

"You don't need to promise me anything." It sounded false even as she said it. He didn't owe her explanations, but she wasn't going to be okay with him dating someone else. It was odd to feel so possessive of someone who had never been hers.

"I want to." He squeezed his fingers around hers, his grip warm and comfortable.

It felt reassuring. She wanted it to be reassuring. Crap.

"Karen? I. Want. To." He tugged her to a stop and turned to face her full on. "If I'm going to flirt with anyone, it's going to be you."

"Me?"

"Yeah. You're kinda cute."

"I'm not twenty."

He shrugged. "Neither am I."

"How old are you, anyway?" Nerves pushed her face into a wide, slightly unnatural smile.

He chuckled. "Thirty-seven."

"Wow, you're old. Der. Older, I mean!" She grimaced. "Than I thought you were. Thirty-seven is...nice."

"Nice."

She nodded.

"Is nice a euphemism for boring?"

She shook her head. "Experienced."

Paul closed the gap between their bodies and trailed his lips along her jaw. As far as first kisses went, that was quick and unexpected. And it blew her socks off. A peck on the cheek. Good grief. She lifted her hand and pressed her fingers to the spot, still feeling remnant tingles.

"If we weren't on the street right now, that would have been on your mouth. And your neck, and maybe your chest—"

She didn't give him a chance to finish the list before she wrapped her arms around his neck and placed her own chaste kiss on his throat. A growl beneath her lips told her that it had the same effect as his kiss had on her.

"Then let's get inside," she murmured in his ear.

He spun on his heel, linking his fingers into hers and taking off down the block, covering the last few steps at a trot. "Your house or mine?"

"Mine's fine," she breathed.

"Deal," he muttered, and turned abruptly onto her walk. "Keys?"

She jangled them and he stepped out of the way, only to move closer again once she was at the door. He pressed in tight behind her, running his hands up and down her sides, and she shivered on the upstroke. The door flung open in front of them and they stumbled inside.

"So," she said. "We're alone."

"We are." He smiled, a look full of anticipation and promise.

She stepped toward him and traced the side of his face with her hand. "I like your smile." She loved it, but she didn't want to scare the guy off. "It changes your entire face from scary cop to awesome dad."

"If you don't mind, I don't really want to think about either of those things right now." He cupped her face.

There was a warning to heed in those words, but he was a big boy. If he wanted this tonight, she wasn't going to be the voice of reason, not when she didn't agree with the reason to begin with.

"I just want..." He lowered his face to hers, close enough to feel his breath on her lips. "I've wanted to kiss you since the first time I saw you."

"The first time we met, or the first time we talked?" She feathered her lips over his in invitation.

"In a minute, you're going to tell me what the difference is. But right now, shut up." He swallowed her protesting yelp, his lips firm and intent against hers. He tasted like beer and smelled like soap, and this should have been just like all the other first kisses in her life, but it wasn't.

It was transcendent.

The tingling sensation he'd started on her jaw now spread over her entire body, and as his fingers stroked back into her hair they left raw lines of awareness on her skin. His mouth opened against hers and his teeth nipped at her bottom lip, causing her to whimper and press closer. *Again*, she pleaded in her head, and he laved that spot with his tongue before repeating the tease. This time, it was her tongue that darted out to salve the swollen lip, and then past it, into his mouth. He rocked back, bending his knees to keep them at the same height, letting her weight lean fully against his body, and when he cupped her bottom and aligned them just so, she found proof that he was as affected by the kiss as she was.

"Wow," she whispered.

"Do you have a couch?" he asked, his breath ragged and uneven against her cheek.

She nodded and stepped back, finding both of his hands with hers so she could stay connected as she led him into the living room.

When the back of her calves bumped into the overstuffed sofa, she paused and reached up to cup Paul's face in her hands. "Hi," she breathed.

"Hi." His hands were strong and warm against her waist, then her hip and her side and up into her hair and down to her bottom all at the same time.

"How many hands do you have?" She murmured the question against his questing mouth as they tumbled to cushions.

"Not nearly enough." His tongue found hers and conversation was abandoned as they lost themselves in the taste of each other. She couldn't help but crawl into his lap, hungry for more of him. He dominated the kiss, even from below, and she let him lead, but took every opportunity he offered to give back in earnest delight.

An unspoken understanding passed between them that they were going to stick to above their clothes petting, and after a time their kisses slowed, turning languid and bone-meltingly sweet. They exchanged innocent, amazing little touches, a hot press of a palm against her side, branding her through her t-shirt, which she returned against his chest, feeling the thump of his heartbeat against her fingers. His remarkably steady, calm heartbeat. For a guy so conflicted about letting loose, he seemed quite at ease with what they were doing.

And why shouldn't he? She'd done everything she could to be non-threatening. While she really wanted to rip off his shirt and lick him from collarbone to navel, because frankly, they were adults, and with all the tax-paying, overtime-working, community-involvement responsibilities that entails, shouldn't they be able to enjoy the one big benefit—an unencumbered social life?

Of course, that led her in the direction of guys like Blake. No, thanks. Not anymore. A dangerous hope flickered in her tummy at the idea that Paul was different. She pushed back at her subconscious. He was different alright, but not in a good way. Well, this was pretty good. Amazing, even. But while Paul wasn't a friends with benefits type of guy, he wasn't a more than friends option either. He was just a friend. With whom she was going to get one delicious night of kissing and petting, to fuel a future of fond fantasies. Nothing more. If she let her gut wander away with hope of anything else, her heart would soon hear of the idea, and then it would all be over.

"You're thinking again." Paul traced the ridge of her earlobe with his tongue. He'd slipped sideways and was now lying on the couch, holding her firmly on top of him, stretched out against his hard, lean frame.

She propped herself up on his chest, trying to ignore how the movement pressed their hips together. "I'm not sure how I feel about being so transparent to you."

He ground his erection into her belly. "I think it's going both ways right now, don't you?"

She couldn't help but smile. There was no doubting the level of physical attraction between them. "Yeah, but that's just one facet of you. You have a central tap into my brain."

He kissed the end of her nose and regarded her face with careful perusal for a moment before responding. "I just know that it's working. I really can't read your thoughts. But I'd like to."

No, you wouldn't. He'd run away screaming if he knew the thoughts that flickered around the edges of her mind. The picket fence possibilities that she couldn't help but envision. And wasn't that reason enough to call it a night and head back to reality. If they could. She might not be able to read all of his thoughts, but the turmoil roiling inside her was clearly reflected in his stormy grey eyes. That was an unguarded depth she'd never seen before, in his eyes, or anyone else's, and it both scared and thrilled her.

Maybe the friend zone was a better place to be. Easier, anyway.

"Karen?"

"What did you say before? Shut up and kiss me, right?" She offered what she hoped came off as an easygoing smirk.

He furrowed his brow. "Hard to argue with that, but—"

She cut him off with a hard press of her lips, tracing the seam of his with the tip of her tongue. He let her in with a groan, and she willed her mind to fade to black.

6

———

THE quiet hum of fluorescent overhead lights was a subtle soundtrack for the moment she said goodbye to a lifelong dream. She'd always liked the Essex library, bigger, more modern than the Wardham location, but at that moment, it felt like hell.

Karen shifted her hips in the wooden chair and wondered if it would be poor form to just leave. The human resources coordinator had all but said that the positions were reserved for graduates of a Master's program. She'd used phrases like *competitive marketplace* and *rapidly evolving field,* and interspersed them with polite smiles and kind words about her experience, but Karen knew a brush-off when she experienced it.

Now she was waiting in the hall like a high school junior caught skipping class, listening to the occasional squeak of the restocking cart and wondering if she could chain herself to it in protest. Except then the books wouldn't be returned to their rightful homes, and that just wouldn't do.

That she wanted to shift from managing inventory at a grocery store to basically the same thing at a library was not lost on her. If anything, it proved that the new Wardham library would be the perfect place for her—no one else would care as much. But apparently passion didn't rate for bupkis in a competitive marketplace. Bah.

"Ms. Miller?" The petite ice queen in a pastel pink twinset stood in front her, a manila envelope in her outstretched hand. "Here's the package on internships I mentioned. Something to consider."

Karen nodded numbly and stood to accept the package. And run away. Bittersweet tears burned at the back of her eyelids and thick emotion clogged her throat. Thirty-four years old and her only option was an internship.

Not the only option. Until the other night, she'd been ready to pack up and move to London or Toronto to study Library Sciences again. And she still was. As she pushed through the double glass doors at the front of the non-descript mid-century single story municipal building that housed the Essex Central Library, Karen recommitted to herself that she wasn't going to limit herself to jobs in Wardham. Not for the town, and not for Paul.

Definitely not for Paul. She paused in the bright sunlight and pressed her fingers to her lips. A shiver trembled through her at the memory of his kiss. His hands, firm and warm and oh so talented. They'd necked on her couch for almost two hours, and it had been one of the most satisfying sexual experiences in her life. Quite something, given the lack of orgasms. At one point she'd been tempted to grind against him, knowing it wouldn't take much to get herself off, but something held her back.

Something smart, because when they walked to the door, bittersweet longing hung over them like a funeral shroud and Karen knew that if they'd gone any further, she wouldn't have recovered. Wouldn't have been able to look Paul in the eye and promise that she understood that night couldn't lead to anything else.

And she'd been fine. Really, truly fine.

Until today.

Mildred had set up this meeting for her, and Karen was appreciative, but she hadn't needed the extra dose of reality. Not this week. She already got it—this was karma for three decades of taking the easy path through life.

She slid her sunglasses on and remotely unlocked her car. At least it was a nice day to roll the windows down and turn up the radio. A grin curled up her face as she moved toward the Camaro. If nothing else went her way, at least she had a wicked ride.

You and me against the world, Hermoine. Her brothers hated the name. No amount of justification stemmed the ribbing, but she didn't care. Her car was fearless, brave and bold. And she wasn't embarrassed about the fangirl naming decision.

As she trailed her fingers along the curve of the front hood, a sweet caress for her baby in advance of the goodness about to happen on the drive home, a faint trill sounded from inside her bag. A text message. She slid the phone out and warily eyed the screen. She hadn't told anyone about the appointment, and she doubted Mildred would betray her confidence.

You can do anything. Believe in yourself.

A random message from a random number. There was no hyperlink, but it read like spam. She'd gotten a few of those the previous year, and put herself on the no-call list. Apparently, that no longer mattered to telemarketers and phishers. *Delete.*

The phone and her bag stashed on the floor of the passenger side, Karen smoothly shifted into reverse and peeled out of the parking space.

The fifteen minute drive down the county road back to Wardham took the edge off her mood, and she considered turning east and heading along the lakeshore for a while, but her pointy toed heels were pinching, so she headed home.

As she screeched into the driveway, not going too fast but not being cautious either, she belatedly realized that Paul was in his backyard. He shot her a furrowed brow look, which promptly restored all grumpiness that had dissolved on the drive. She didn't need any judgment on her driving today. Or ever, but definitely not today.

And definitely not from Paul. Their lives couldn't—wouldn't—mix, so he could take his thoughts and stuff them.

He moved toward her, but she waved him off with a snarky, "Sorry, Constable."

She stomped inside, regret niggling at the back of her head as she caught sight of his shocked expression. It wasn't fair to take out her frustration on him. She'd have to find a way to apologize later. *Without throwing yourself at him or sticking your tongue down his throat.*

She'd barely made it through the kitchen when her phone rang. She yanked it out of her bag without so much as glancing at the screen. Enough with people already. "What?"

"I like your skirt."

She whirled around and peered through the window. "Uh, hi?"

He raised his hand.

"What are you doing?"

"Talking to you."

"On the phone?"

"I thought it would be safer than approaching in person."

"I've had a bad day." She turned away from the window and headed for the stairs. She'd wanted to change into comfy pants since she'd left Essex.

"Do you want to talk about it?"

She stopped at the top of the stairs and dropped her head. "No." It came out as half word, half groan. And it wasn't really true. Ignoring everything else that was or wasn't going on between them, Paul was surprisingly the one person with whom she felt safe sharing her secrets. "Yes, but not right now. Are you going to be around later? We could have a beer and commiserate on how much life sucks."

"I've got a shift tonight."

"Oh." Hot pressure built behind her eyes and she swiped furiously at her lids, refusing the tears. For any reason, but definitely not because he wasn't available for a backyard chat. That was ridiculous. She thought about turning around and going back outside for a few minutes, just to see him, but she wasn't sure that wouldn't just feed the monster inside her who wanted all that could not be had.

"You're not at the window anymore. Where'd you go?"

Fantasyland. "Upstairs. I'm done with the fancy clothes." If she hadn't been so wrapped up in grumpiness, she might have noticed his silence right away, but her blouse was half unbuttoned before she realized Paul hadn't responded. "You still there?"

He cleared his throat. "Yep."

"Distract me. Tell me something interesting."

"Uhm…I can't think of anything right now."

"Oh. Do you need to get back to your yard work? I can let you go—"

"No." He interjected quickly enough that she stopped what she was doing and sat down on her bed. "Hang on a second, I just need to wash my hands."

A screen door clapped shut, then the white noise of running water obscured everything else. She lay back on the bed and kicked first one heel across the room, then the other.

"You still there?" Out of breath and deeper than usual, his voice vibrated through the phone and straight to her core.

She pressed her eyes shut and willed herself not to drift again. "Mmm-hmm."

"Would you rather hear about Megan's science project, or the grow-op bust that was actually an oregano farm?"

Warm relief washed over her. "Both. Oregano farm first."

He chuckled and launched into his story, pausing from time to time when she laughed, or asked a question.

It didn't take long to sink into the conversation as they traded warm murmurs back and forth, and at the next natural lull, she took a deep breath. "Thank you."

"For what?"

"Distracting me. I don't even need to change into my comfy clothes now."

"You didn't get changed?"

"I started to, got halfway undressed, but then I gave up and lay down." This time, she caught on to his silence right away, and flushed a deep scarlet as she rewound her words and realized what she'd just shared. "Uhm, was that too much information?"

"God, no." She wasn't imagining that husky tone, right? "If there's information I'll always want more of, it's your state of undress in a bedroom." Right.

"That's not friendly."

"Sure it is."

"You know what I mean. It's too friendly."

"Can't help it."

"We can't do this, remember?"

"Talk on the phone? Because that's all we're doing. Talking. No harm in that, right?" His voice was taut with tension, and a challenge. She could handle one night of making out, but ongoing flirting? It hurt her heart that Paul wasn't open to a relationship, but now that wasn't the only barrier. She would probably be leaving town soon. Zero chance of anything happening once Paul knew that fact.

"Right. Just talking."

"About your state of undress." He dropped his voice to a lower register. "I can't get the taste of you out of my mouth, Karen. Have you been thinking about that night?"

Even though there were many walls and a driveway between them, Karen was suddenly very conscious that she was just wearing a bra and a skirt. *And underpants.* She was also quite aware of her underwear. "Uhm, yeah."

"Tell me."

"That was nice...making out."

He chuckled. "It was. You make me want to forget my principles, Karen." The growled words sounded like a compliment, but she wasn't so weak that she couldn't push back at the unintended truth.

"That doesn't sound like a good thing."

"It's not, but you are. Maybe I need to re-evaluate."

Let me know once you've done that, buddy. But she couldn't voice the brush off. She didn't have a co-dependent bone in her body, but something about Paul made her want to promise to wait. Made her want to accept whatever half-measures he could handle. Except she probably wouldn't be around when he sorted his shit out. "Let's not make this complicated. Can we go back to talking about making out?"

"We can start there." His voice was silky, pure sex in her ear, and she found herself holding her breath. *And then go where?* "Tell me what you're wearing."

"A skirt."

"I saw it. Very pretty. Can you spread your legs in it?"

Oh god. "Uhm, no."

"Take it off."

She tucked the phone tight under her chin and rolled to the side so she could grab the zipper in the back. After laying the skirt over her footboard, she scrambled up to the head of the bed and fluffed up a couple of pillows to recline against. "Okay."

"I love the little panting noises you were making as you did that, Karen." His words dripped over her skin like sweet oil. "Listening to you made me hard."

"Really?"

"Yes, really." He sounded amused, but in a way that included her. "Everything about you turns me on."

"Wow. Okay, I like that."

"Good. Are you wearing anything else?"

"A bra and…panties. They match."

"Describe them."

"They're pink, pale pink, and mostly see-through." She paused as he groaned and shifted. He was right. The little noises were awesome. "The underwear are bikini style, so they just have little straps on the sides. The bra is a demi-cup—"

"Off. Take them off." The words came out strangled and her heart swelled at the effect she was having on him. "Wait. Just the bra. Leave the panties on. I want your hand inside them. Imagine the fabric pressing against your skin is my hand guiding you."

Her bra sailed across the room and she wiggled into the center of the bed, pausing for a second to put her phone on speaker. "Guiding me to do what?"

"First, we're going to find out if you're wet. Are you wet for me, darlin'?" If she wasn't already—which she totally was—she would be after that question.

"Yes." Her answer came out in a breathless rush.

"One hand in your panties, the other cupping a breast. Don't touch your nipples yet."

She wasn't going to, that wasn't something she would normally do when touching herself, but as soon as he gave that directive, she was suddenly aware of both nipples, her areolas pebbling and the dark pink tips jutting sharply toward the ceiling. She licked her lips, imagining him above her, propped up on his forearms, gazing at her breasts. She plumped up her left breast, offering him a taste. Her right hand, previously nestled on top of her pubic hair, now drifted lower to press on her sex. "What are you doing?"

"I've got my eyes closed. One hand on my cock, moving up and down, nice and slow, the other holding this phone so hard it might just break."

She shifted her head to look at her bedroom wall. Thirty feet separated their bare skin. "Are you imagining that it's me touching you?"

"Not right now. I've had that fantasy before, though. We're in the shower. You wrap your fingers around me until I come all over your stomach. But right now, I'm there, in your bedroom, standing at the foot of your bed, watching you touch yourself."

"I want you on top of me."

"I'll get there. Right now I want your legs as wide as they can get. You've got the longest legs. They're so hot. I get distracted every time I see you in shorts, thinking about them wrapped around my waist."

Her pussy clenched under her roving fingers. She needed to buy more shorts.

"I'm looking at you now. In my head, you're not wearing anything, and I can see how wet you are." She gasped at the picture he was painting. She wasn't a virgin, not by a long shot, but to the best of her recollection, no one had ever looked at her spread eagle on a bed. If anyone else had suggested it, she'd be mortified. But Paul…his appraisal would be heated and wonderful. He'd make sure to reward her vulnerability. And she'd be able to watch him, watching her. See how it affected him.

"What do you look like?" She was most definitely in an altered state if she was blithely asking him to describe his erection. "I know what it feels like, but…we've never seen each other naked."

"My cock? It's…I don't know, it's a cock. It's hard. The head is dark red, almost purple, and right now it's throbbing to be inside you."

She seriously might faint before this was over. "Nice. I'd like to see it."

"I'd like that too. I could come ov—"

"No! Not…not today. This is probably where we should…you know. Be reasonable. Have boundaries."

"Okay. But we're not done here."

"We're not?" Oh thank god.

"Don't you want to come? I know I do. I want to come all over you."

Yes, please.

"Can you get yourself off with your fingers?"

She nodded dumbly before remembering he couldn't see her. "Yeah. Yes, I can." Another first for discussion. Another moment lacking embarrassment.

"Then do it. You wanted me on top of you, darlin', remember? That's where I am. I crawled onto the bed with you, and now I'm between your legs, your fingers on your clit, dipping lower when you need a bit more to keep it smooth and easy, and my hand is right next to yours. I'm fisting my cock against your hip, and our knuckles bump as we get faster and faster."

A helpless moan escaped her lips as she picked up speed, matching his fantasy. "Why aren't you inside me? I want you to…"

"Want me to what? Say it, Karen."

"I want you to fuck me."

"I will, but not today. The first time I'm inside you, it's going to be for real. Nothing is going to be left to fantasy. You'll see all of me and I'll see all of you, and this will pale in comparison. When we fuck, and that's a when, Karen, not an if, because I need you. When we fuck, it's going. To. Be. Real."

His strained staccato words tipped her over the top, her fingers a blur as she gasped a final breath before pure pleasure wracked through her body, leaving her boneless and twitching on the bed. The echo of his voice rang in her ears, his heavy breathing proof that they'd done him in as well. "Oh my god."

"Yeah." A long pause pulsed between them. "You okay?"

"I think so." She twisted to her side, tugging the blanket with her, cocooning her naked body. "Yes. I'm okay."

"I have to go to work soon. What are you doing tomorrow? Can we have breakfast before I go to sleep?"

If she thought too hard about any of what just happened, or what was to come in the future, she'd lose the warm muzzy feeling she was currently luxuriating in, so she let her heart answer instead of her head. "I'd like that. I'll be up early, come by when your shift is over."

7

S EVEN a.m. arrived not a minute too soon. He'd responded to a domestic violence call shortly after midnight that turned into an all-nighter at Emergency in Essex, waiting for a rape kit to be processed so he could take it back to the station. He was still an unknown quantity to the local medical departments and victim support services, which didn't help given that the victim involved was mightily pissed off at him. Her ex-husband was claiming she'd hit him with a heavy bookend, which constituted a weapon, and was claiming she struck first. None of it was good, some of it was truly awful, and because he had to explore all of it, he probably hadn't done enough to acknowledge the awful.

He didn't shy away from complicated, and he knew his role—collect evidence and information to build a file, and possibly a case or cases, as warranted. At the end of the day, or night in this case, as long as he acted appropriately, it didn't matter if anyone liked him. But it was a long, quiet night of harsh looks as people came and went from the exam room. The woman had made it clear she didn't want him there, she wanted someone else to transport the rape kit, but there wasn't anyone else available.

In the end, she'd listened to a nurse practitioner who found the right words to explain the importance of chain of custody, and shortly before dawn Paul headed back to Wardham with a sealed cardboard box.

Waiting in the antiseptic corridor on a vinyl padded chair had given him plenty of time to replay the unexpected encounter with Karen from the previous day. He'd done a lot of fantasizing about what sex with her might be like, but the real thing, albeit across a driveway and through a phone line, was hotter than he imagined. But that wasn't where his thoughts ended up in the middle of the night, surrounded by the proof that life can sometimes veer horribly off-track. That people can damage each other. Goodness was fleeting, and he'd touched goodness now more than once. It was time to stop pretending that he wasn't lucky for it. Time to stop testing the stretch of that luck.

He was no stranger to dirty sex. For a long time, it was the only kind of sex he had. After Susan, he hadn't wanted another serious relationship, and nothing advertised that a hookup was casual better than being explicit about carnal intent.

But yesterday had been almost exactly the reverse. The harder each of them pushed against their growing attraction, the tighter the web around them gathered. There was nothing casual about his feelings toward Karen. He wasn't delusional—there were still significant road blocks to his life being relationship-friendly. But he was tired of pretending that he didn't want more of her. Her mouth, to start with. Her heart and mind, too. Her body, wrapped around his, and not just for a night.

Dating. He thought he'd sworn it off forever, but Karen was different. They'd have to take it slow, and he'd need to make it clear up front that Megan-time was sacred, but that wouldn't be a problem. She'd probably kneecap him for thinking otherwise.

He was grinning as he changed at the station, enough so that the desk clerk commented on his mood as he headed out to his car. He just waved and kept going. It probably wouldn't take long for the entire town to find out about their relationship, but he wasn't giving anyone a head start with the gossip.

The shit-eating grin didn't waver as he quietly pulled into

their shared drive and parked his car in his garage. It was inevitable that they'd meet, being neighbours, but he was glad he'd parked between their houses long enough to rile her up. The image of her striding toward him, arms streaked with dirt, sun glinting off her mahogany hair, breasts bouncing lightly under her t-shirt, would always make him smile. A woman on a mission. She had no idea how determined she could be. How fierce.

He thought about dashing into his house and having a quick shower, but he was bagged. He didn't want a quick fuck with Karen. Well, he did, and would always, but not today. Not their first time. He wanted to share a cup of coffee with her, and soak in her goodness, and then crawl into bed and recharge so they could have a real date that night. Maybe crack open the box of condoms he'd bought last week. The box he'd he told himself he wasn't going to need. *Liar.*

He rapped twice on her back door and stretched his arm up high, resting his forearm against the frame, so when she opened the door and stepped forward, she was close enough to catch around the waist and he pulled her tight against him. "Hey, darlin'."

"Hi, you." She tilted her face toward his, which didn't take much, as their bodies aligned perfectly. "You coming in?"

"In a minute. First…good morning." He drifted the tip of his nose against hers, relishing the slow smile that crawled across her face before he lowered his mouth to cover hers. She tasted like orange juice, and the pure greatness of that almost brought him to his knees. He threaded his free hand into her curls and lost himself in all that was soft. Her hair, her mouth, the swell of her hip under his other hand. It was all just exactly what he wanted. What he needed.

"Long night?" Karen whispered the question against his face, seemingly happy to stay wrapped in his arms in her doorway. He nodded and she buried her face in his neck, transferring her happy morning warmth to him. "I've got coffee, or I can make tea if you'll have trouble falling asleep?"

He squeezed her hip and signaled that they could move inside. "Fifteen years of shift work. I don't have any problem falling asleep. Coffee would be great."

He told her what he could about his shift, which wasn't much, and she brought him a steaming mug and the carton of milk from the fridge. She confessed she had been ignoring his text messages, thinking they were random spam. When he made a face at the idea his texts were so generic, she reached across the table and squeezed his hand. He twisted his palm so their fingers interlaced. Her fingertips teased at his knuckles, but he felt that barest of touches like a direct caress against his groin.

Meeting her gaze wasn't any better. She was throwing off pheromones and heat all over the place. He'd put that chemistry to good use later. "I was thinking you could come over to my place later to watch a movie."

"That's as good a cover story as any, I guess." She giggled so hard she snorted, and then blushed. He loved all of that, but he was serious about the movie.

"I'm not going to deny that after we watch a film, I'm going to do my best to get you naked and in my bed. That's going to happen. But I also want to spend time with you."

She narrowed her gaze, like she was trying to parse what he said for hidden meaning. Jesus, why was it such a foreign concept to her that she was desirable? Worthy of dating? Totally and utterly wantable?

"Is it me?" He teased, but maybe she really didn't want to date him. "Are you afraid I only watch zombie movies?"

"Zombies would be okay. A reason to cuddle, anyway." A tentative smile. "Although I'd rather watch an action flick, or a classic Bond film, something like that."

"So it's a date?"

"It's a plan, anyway."

They'd work on the language later. He'd get creative in ways to convince her it was a date. Hands-on creative. But now wasn't the time, not while she was being skittish, so he turned his attention to the milk carton on the table. He would have thought she'd be a ceramic milk pitcher person. He liked that she wasn't, or at least wasn't with him. "Do you have a matching sugar and creamer set?"

She shot him a startled look. "Sure…do you want to use it?"

An honest to goodness belly laugh rippled out from his core, and he pulled her around the table and into his lap. "God, no. I was just thinking…it doesn't matter. Come here, kiss me again."

She did, but then she pulled back and pinned him under a challenging gaze. "I still want to know."

"I like that you don't think of me as a guest."

Her face softened. In a big way. "Yeah. I don't. That's weird, huh?"

He shrugged. "It's good. It means this is something real."

If she wasn't right in front of him, close enough to count the freckles on her nose, he would have missed the barest flare in her eyes, and the slight intake of air.

"What?"

She shifted uncomfortably on his lap. "This is something real?"

Frustration swelled in his chest, and he tamped it down. He'd had a long night. He didn't need to take that out on Karen. "Yeah. Isn't it?"

"I thought…" Her face crumpled for a moment before she found her strength. "We don't know each other that well, yet, but I'm pretty sure you've been giving me clear signals that you aren't available."

"What about yesterday?" He chose his words carefully. They just needed to have a conversation and get on the same page. More information would resolve this problem. He *had* been sending mixed signals, she wasn't wrong about that.

"It was nice." *Nice?* He wanted to interject that he didn't need to be in the same room to know that it had blown her away, but she looked so uncertain he didn't dare. "But just like the night we walked home from Danny's, I thought it was a one-time thing."

"I told you it wasn't."

"I thought that was just…"

"Just what?"

"You know…sexy talk." She was still in his lap, but her body language was clear. She was slipping away from him, putting up a wall. How could he explain that she didn't need to protect herself from him?

"I don't have phone sex with just anyone." From the look on her face, that didn't help. He cursed under his breath. "And I came over for breakfast. We're making plans for tonight. What's going on here, Karen?"

She reached up and stroked his cheek briefly before pushing to a stand and turning away from him. She propped her hands on her hips and stared out the kitchen window that overlooked their driveway.

"You've got too much on the line to risk a new relationship."

There was no controlling his frustration at that. That was his decision to make. "You have no idea about what's on the line." He surged out of his seat and paced toward her, stopping just short of touching her back. Her back was straight, too straight, and he was close enough to see the firm set of her jaw. "And that's not the real reason you're throwing up a road block here."

"Then what's changed between last week and this morning? Your ex isn't going to give you a hard time about dating again?"

"She shouldn't."

"She will."

"I'll make her understand. Megan thinks you're great. She never liked any of my—"

"You really don't need to finish that statement." Karen whirled around, but she crossed her arms over her heaving chest, making it clear her attention wasn't going to be positive. "Why can't this just be something casual? Private?"

"It can be private. But darlin', despite your current apparent dislike for me, what we have…there's nothing casual about it."

He stepped into her personal space, crowding her against the counter. "Did you think I wanted to be fuck buddies?"

She blanched, but didn't break eye contact. After a loaded moment, she relaxed her arms and placed one hand lightly against his chest. Her expression didn't change, though. "If I did, that was clearly a mistake. But that was all that would ever be possible between us." Her voice dropped to a broken whisper. "You've been up for a long time. This has gotten heavier than it needed to. Maybe you should just go."

He shook his head. Her words sounded reasonable, but her tone was...destroyed. And it ripped through his chest like a blade. "I don't understand." His own voice rasped with emotion, surprising himself, and from her wide eyes, Karen too. "Are you breaking up with me?"

She laughed without humour. "Not possible to break up what's never been together."

No. He wouldn't accept that. "Say whatever you want about the future, but we've been together, Karen." He didn't move, but he was going to, unless she gave him a sign he shouldn't. "Do I need to remind you?"

She stared at him, mere inches between them, and slowly shook her head from side to side.

"No, I don't. But I'm going to." He moved slowly, giving her time to stop him. She didn't. His feet bracketed hers, and his hands cupped her face as he took her mouth hungrily, stroking deep with his tongue, staking a claim that rejected false barriers. He poured more than a month of desire and fantasies into the kiss, letting hunger set the pace, not caring that it wasn't suave or seductive.

Fuck, if she was done with him, she'd know that he hadn't been done with her. Not by a long shot. He needed her, and not her body. He needed her heart and her friendship, and she didn't get that at all. He was the furthest thing from an ideal boyfriend, but he'd have made it work. Somehow.

"Paul. Paul, stop." He barely heard it, but as the word registered in his brain, he jerked away. He shook his head and stepped back, still breathing hard.

"I'm sorry," he muttered.

Karen pressed her fingers to her mouth and shook her head slowly. "No, don't be. That was…I know, okay? I feel it…but I need to tell you…"

A lone tear rolled down her cheek, and if he was capable of tears, he'd probably have a matching one. This was not how the morning should have gone. "What? Tell me what?"

"I'm probably going to…" She swallowed hard and stood straighter. With a deep breath, she steadied her voice. "My adventure. Remember? It's going to take me away from Wardham. At the end of the summer, I'll be heading somewhere, wherever I can get into a Library Science program. I started to explore the options last week, and my meeting yesterday cemented this decision."

She was leaving.

He hadn't seen that coming.

"Right." She had been, after all. His life was already fractured enough. He couldn't add a long distance relationship to it, not without impacting Megan. Not without threatening his tenuous custody agreement. Susan would have a shit-fit if he spent a significant amount of time… "Where would you go?"

"I don't know. Toronto, maybe London. Might have to go elsewhere in the province. It depends which program would have space for me at this late date. It's well past the application window. But I don't want to wait another year." Her lips curved south in a helpless frown. "I need to do this, Paul."

He knew that. And he was rapidly understanding that it didn't make her happy, but neither would staying here and working at the store for the next twenty years.

"I'll be back."

He nodded. There wasn't anything left to say.

"We could—"

"No." He sounded brusque and heartless. That was a reasonable cover for heartbroken. "We can't. It's better this way." He stepped backward slowly, his gaze never leaving her face. He wanted to soak up this last private moment. He wouldn't be getting another one. "I'll see you around, Karen."

As he stepped out to the deck and down the stairs toward his own house, her quiet sobs echoed in the early morning still. He almost turned back, but he was pretty sure he'd done enough damage that he wouldn't be welcome in her kitchen again.

8

HEARTBREAK made mincemeat of indecision. Within a few days, Karen had found three programs that would accept a late application from her, and informed her parents of her plan to leave in August for a year. Functionally, this meant they needed to make a permanent decision about what to do with the store, because when, or if, she returned, it would be for a librarian position. She'd paid a high enough price for this adventure, she was damned sure she'd see it through to the end and make that sacrifice worthwhile.

"Earth to Karen. Come in—"

"Leave her alone, Carrie." Evie Calhoun leaned over the back of their friend's couch and gave her a smothering hug.

Karen flashed them both a half-hearted smile. "I'm sorry, I'm not being very good company."

"Meh, we all have days like that." Evie clambered over the couch and bounced into the seat next to Carrie. Karen shook her head at her friend's energy. She needed to do more Pilates and fewer pints of ice cream. "Want to talk about it?"

"Nope."

Carrie narrowed her eyes and ignored the answer. "So if you don't want to talk about it, it could be work. Unless it's personal…

guy trouble?" Karen froze. Her best friend was way too smart for her own good. "Oooh--!"

"It's work," she quickly interjected. "I guess you'll hear about it soon enough. I'm heading back to school."

She outlined the tentative plan, glossing over what sparked her into action. After briefly outlining the pros and cons of the different schools she'd applied to, she reached for her wine glass and settled back into her seat for their reactions.

Her friends exchanged a long look, then turned and pinned her with identical skeptical expressions.

"So, first you don't want to talk about it," Evie started.

"And then you talk about it." Carrie crossed her arms over her chest. "Honey, do we look new?"

"No?"

"No. What else is going on? The last few days you've been miserable. We didn't call an emergency girls' night so we could drink wine."

"You don't even have a reaction to me moving away?"

"Are you going to stay away?"

"No." They exchanged smiles loaded with understanding and relief. "Thanks."

Evie leaned across the coffee table and tapped Karen's foot. "Spill."

She couldn't. Where to start? Where to end? None of what happened with Paul made sense to her, how could she explain it to anyone else? "I did something stupid, I guess. It's not a big deal, except it might have been a big deal and I didn't realize."

Carrie opened a drawer in the coffee table and pulled out another bottle of wine and a spare corkscrew. "We've got emergency supplies, we're good. Start at the beginning."

By the time she'd caught them up to date on most of the details, leaving out only the bits about Paul's life that she didn't feel were hers to share, her friends' expressions no longer matched.

"I don't understand. So he wants to have a relationship. Why wouldn't you just date until you leave?" Evie shook her head. "Maybe it's my utter lack of a sex life talking, but I think you made a mountain out of a molehill."

"No, you did the right thing." Carrie pursed her lips. "I've seen you two together. You like him. No way would you end up leaving at the end of the summer."

Karen couldn't help but protest. "Hey, I'm not a brainless bimbo." But Carrie wasn't wrong. "I'd leave. But I'd be miserable. And I'm not sure I wouldn't come home early again."

Both women knew how Karen had ended up managing the grocery store. "You wouldn't." Evie shook her head violently. "You're a different person now. You know what you want."

Karen glanced at Carrie, but her friend was studiously filling her wine glass. Not saying anything. She wanted to ask why. But a bigger part of her was afraid of Carrie's honest opinion, so she silently slid her own glass across the coffee table and shifted the conversation. "Don't you have the boys this weekend? Don't get me wrong, I appreciate the company, but...?" Girls' nights were almost always called on Saturdays when Evie's ex-husband had their two boys.

"I'm going out of town next weekend. I got a smokin' deal on a train and hotel deal, so I'm going to Toronto for a couple of days of culture that I can't get in this backwards hick town." Evie managed to say the last bit with a straight face, but her voice was softer than usual. It wasn't the town she needed a break from. Karen grabbed her friend's wine glass and shoved it toward Carrie. Top-ups needed all round.

They drank in silence for a couple of minutes, giving Evie the space she needed. She'd share when she could, and it didn't take long. "Dale's introducing the kids to his girlfriend while I'm away. And she's sleeping at his house, so they're going to play happy family for 48 hours. I haven't gotten laid in two years, and he's managed to move on full-circle."

Shit. Karen hated that she'd been so buried in her own feelings that she hadn't realized her friend was hurting. "How long have they been together?"

Evie shrugged. "A couple of months. It's not her. Or him. It's just that I'm frozen in the moment after I left him, and it's time for a thaw."

"You should take your own advice. Have some fun. Hook up with some big city cutie, love him and leave him." Karen took a big slug of wine. The more she drank, the better a one night stand sounded. "That's what I wanted to do with Paul."

"Maybe he'll come around. Living next door to you would test any man's resolve."

Carrie stood up. "If Evie gets any drunker, I think you could probably have a one night stand with her."

"Hey!" The pretty blond shrugged. "Yeah, you probably could."

"Great, so the list of people who would do me is a whopping two."

Carrie and Evie exchanged a look that Karen was either too drunk or too stupid to understand.

"What?"

"That's seriously how you see yourself?" Carrie rolled her eyes and headed for the kitchen.

"Hey!" Karen stumbled to her feet. "I get that I'm drunk, and a bit self-centered today, but are you being bitchy with me?"

Instead of answering, the redhead stepped out of view, muttering under her breath.

"Seriously, is she mad at me?"

Evie raggedly shook her head from side to side. "Nah. She just doesn't approve of casual sex."

"I'm the furthest thing from a prude!" This was shouted from the kitchen. Karen decided to ignore all comments that weren't offered in a social fashion.

"Maybe she's not getting enough at home." Instead of offending Carrie, this just got a sarcastic laugh. "Oh crap, that's her point, isn't it? That we should be looking for variations on Ian?"

Evie drained her wine glass. "She wouldn't be wrong, you know. Nixon men are good stock. Kyle has made my sister very happy." Carrie's brother-in-law had recently proposed to Evie's sister. Proof that Wardham was too small and Karen needed to get out in order to find a life worth living. "But good men are hard to find."

Carrie popped back into the room at that. "That's not true. They're out there, but you can't..." She waved at the two of them, at a loss for words. After thinking for a minute, she stabbed a finger in the air at Karen. "You're so convinced that no one wants you, and you have no idea how gorgeous you are. And when you meet someone who doesn't just like you, but *likes* you, you run scared at the first disagreement." Karen opened her mouth to protest, but Carrie was on a roll. She turned toward Evie. "And you! You're in the prime of your life. You're right, it's time to thaw, but don't sell yourself short either. You deserve a good time *and* a good friend."

"Baby steps. First the good time. It's been so long, I may have forgotten what to do," the blond muttered, skepticism all over her face.

"Not all men are as selfish as Dale, sweetie." Over the years, Evie had shared enough about her ex that Karen knew this needed to be said, but she was glad that Carrie was the one speaking the truth. Her relationship with Ian wasn't perfect, but it was clear that man adored his wife and treated her like a queen. For years Karen had thought he was one of a kind. Her closest male friends, other than Ian, had spent most of their twenties proving that fact. Ian's brother Kyle had recently rekindled a long ago relationship with his first love, and in his active pursuit of Laney, Karen and many others in Wardham had fallen for him as well. In a totally platonic, happy for them both kind of way, of course. But before that reunion, Kyle had been just as bad as Dale. Or their friend Ty, who had slept with half the pretty girls between Detroit and Toronto, and was on a mission to bed the other half.

Paul had alluded to a messy past. Enough that his ex-wife would have concerns about any new relationship, which made Karen's stomach pitch wildly. And yet with her, he'd been restrained and sweet. Right up until he got dirty, but even that had been…attentive. He heard her whispered fantasies and delivered. No way would Paul be selfish in the bedroom.

"Care to elaborate about what's putting that look on your face?" Evie looked so keen for something, anything, that Karen didn't want to disappoint.

"Is it possible that the best sex of my life was over the phone?" She let her head fall back against the couch with a small wail. "And I'm never going to have it again?"

"Seriously, it was that good?" Carrie raised her eyebrows. "Maybe you should damn the consequences and go for it."

"It was incredible," Karen whispered. The memory of his voice, his words, flooded her chest with heat. "Uninhibited sex is not a foreign idea to me, but up until last week, it was still just a *concept*, ya know? Now I've tasted it, and I want more."

"We had some knockout moments like that. One night we drank a magnum of champagne and did some unspeakable one-time-only things…I mean, I would have done them again, but Dale never mentioned them…" Evie shrugged. "I guess that's one of the many reasons we're divorced. Couldn't even talk about sex."

Carrie nodded slowly. "Are you sure this isn't just a communication problem with Paul?"

Karen shook her head, misery replacing the temporary wave of desire. "There's more that I can't share, but he's really not open to a casual fling, and I need to respect that."

———

IT WAS LATE by the time Karen got home. Carrie's husband had taken one look at the blushing, giggling women and pronounced none of them fit to drive, which was not a surprise. He loaded Karen and Evie into his truck, pulled his wife in tight for a kiss that bordered on indecent and left no doubt that he was comfortable with the unspeakable things. Ian Nixon was one of the good guys, and he treated his wife right. Karen knew that Carrie was speaking from experience when she suggested communication might be the key—Ian hadn't always been that attentive.

But she couldn't see a way for this situation with Paul to be anything other than heartbreaking. For one or the other, and probably both of them.

She almost climbed into bed in her clothes, but she wouldn't be able to fall asleep without brushing her teeth, and that step in the routine led her to her pajama drawer as if by rote. On autopilot, she padded over to her laptop to check her email. What the hell, she was upright, might as well be thorough.

It took her a few bleary blinks to understand the words swimming on the screen in front of her. After reading the message over a few times, she reached for the phone. Her mother answered on the third ring.

"Karen? Is everything okay?"

"Yep. Sorry, I know it's late."

"That's okay, sweetie."

"I got an email today, probably shoulda been sent to you." Karen blinked again. She was pretty sure she just slurred the last three words together. Crap.

"Honey, are you drunk?"

"Tipsy."

Her mother chuckled in her ear. "Do you want to call me in the morning?"

"Nah, it's okay."

"Uhm, okay…an email, you say?"

"I think it's an offer to buy the store. I dunno, I could be wrong. I am drunk, after all."

9

———

THERE would never be a good time for his ex-wife to visit and pass judgment on his new life, but Paul really wasn't in the mood for it today. Unfortunately, Susan was heading to a cottage not far from Wardham for the weekend, so her offer to drop Megan off was entirely reasonable.

He doubted she'd want to come inside, but vacuumed just in case. Rescued the latest issue of *National Geographic* from the bathroom and set it out on the coffee table. Paced for a while before convincing himself he was being silly. He opened his laptop at the desk under the front window and called up his email. There was a nice note from a student who had volunteered in his department in Windsor, asking for a letter of reference. He appreciated the distraction, and was mid-composition when Susan's hatchback pulled up to the curb.

He stepped out onto his porch and lifted a hand in greeting as she got out. She returned the gesture before reaching into the trunk to grab Megan's backpack. His daughter was already bounding toward him from the curb, and he took the stairs quickly to greet her on the walk with a bone crusher hug.

"Have a good week, sweetie?"

She nodded. "I've got some homework to do, but it's not too bad."

Susan joined them. "Hi, Paul." She flicked her gaze over the small bungalow behind him, then over to Karen's house, and down the street. "Nice neighbourhood. Cute town, too."

"Thanks. It's nice. I like it." *Painfully wonderful* and *am tortured on a daily basis by my proximity to my off-limits neighbour* would probably be too much information.

She handed over a card. "I'm not sure what cell reception is like at the cottage, but they have a landline. Here's the address and phone number. Try my cell first, but just in case…"

He nodded. "You're meeting friends there?" She didn't answer right away and he waved her off. "Sorry, none of my business."

"No, it's fine. Meg, why don't you take your bag inside?"

"Seriously? Mom, you always say that when you want to have an adult conversation." Their daughter rolled her eyes.

"With good reason, kiddo. Listen to your mom and dump your bag, then we'll go for a bike ride. And put the eye roll away, please." He took a deep breath and shared a *What can you do?* look with Susan.

"I know it's normal boundary testing, but holy crap, the attitude!" Susan puffed her cheeks out in frustration. "I appreciate you taking her for the whole weekend."

"It's not a favour. I always want more time with her." He crossed his arms over his chest and slowed his next exhale. This was the first deviation from their revised custody plan, and he couldn't help but get his back up. After four years of only wanting to discuss this through lawyers, he didn't know how to take this long unseen, more flexible, side of Susan.

"I know." She reached out and placed her small manicured hand on his forearm. "But thank you all the same. And about the cottage…I'm meeting a friend there. A man that I've been seeing."

"Has Meg met him yet?"

"Yes, a couple of times. He has two kids, a twelve year old boy and an eight year old girl. We went to the sugar bush together."

Maple syrup season had been over for two months. "That was a while ago."

"We're taking it slow. I want to get it right this time." Paul winced, and she sucked in a breath. "Sorry, that's not what I mean." She squeezed his arm and dropped her hand. "Anyway, I thought you should know."

"Okay, thanks." He meant it. He wanted Susan to know she could share anything that might affect Megan. And he didn't harbour any ill-will toward her, or any lingering feelings, so if she was happy and his daughter's feelings and safety were being considered, that's all that mattered.

The screen door slapped open and Megan stomped across the porch and down the stairs. "Are you guys done fighting?"

"We weren't—"

Paul's protest was cut off as Megan let out a holler and took off past him at a run. "Hey! Karen!"

His heart thudded to a stop and his vision dimmed as Susan tipped her head to the side to better see around him where their daughter was headed. His back was to them, but he could imagine what was happening behind him. Megan, animatedly carrying on about something. Karen, listening, because she would still care about his daughter, and it was probably about books, so she'd care for that reason as well. If she was coming home from work, she'd be in jeans and a polo shirt. Otherwise maybe capris and a t-shirt. Something bright and colourful, because she'd be trying to put on a brave face to the world. He knew what that was like.

"Who's Karen?" Susan tilted her face up to his, and he willed her not to read anything there.

"My neighbour." He pointed to her house. "She manages the grocery store in town."

"Oh right, the cookie making incident! Meg thought that was pretty cool."

"Yeah. They both like books." His voice was way too gruff, but he couldn't help it. Any second now they'd drift into his peripheral vision. He could hear them approaching. Maybe ten feet away. Eight. Aching awareness prickled at the back of his neck and down his spine. Susan was watching him with unabashed curiosity, and he furrowed his brow. The best defense... "She's nice. Not my type, but you know...pleasant."

As soon as the words were out his mouth, he regretted them. They weren't even a little bit true, but Susan seemed to believe them. What did that say about him, that she so readily accepted him as an asshole? Disappointment, probably on behalf of all women everywhere, drifted across her face. In that moment as he turned to introduce Susan to Karen, he needed no more proof of his inability to love than his ex-wife and his fantasy girl standing toe to toe, about to bond over being done with him.

Longing and denied desire shot through his gut before he even saw her, and he had trouble lifting his gaze from the sidewalk, but he couldn't very well introduce Susan to the crack at their feet. He took his time getting there, noting first that she had new sandals, and she'd painted her toenails red, but one had chipped. He wanted to fix that for her. Fuck, he had problems. Nail polish. What the hell?

Her bare calves, already tanned and toned, led to cropped black yoga pants, which hugged her pelvis and sparked unbidden fantasy of what lay underneath. He skipped up to her face, because he was afraid he might get lost around her breasts and embarrass himself more than he probably already had. But as soon as they made eye contact, he wished they hadn't, because lurking under her practiced smile was a shallow pool of pain, so bright and obvious that he almost took a step toward her before he remembered that it wasn't his role to hug her. Not his place to heal the pain he'd inflicted.

And from the wide, panicky look in her eye, some of it was fresh. She'd heard what he said to Susan. Perfect. He took a deep breath. "Karen, this is Megan's mom. Susan, this is Karen. She's... made our move here very easy."

It was weak, but what else could he say? *You could apologize. You could kiss her and damn the consequences.*

Susan extended her hand and the women exchanged pleasantries while they sized each other up. They couldn't be more opposite. Susan had also changed a lot since their marriage. Her blond hair was highlighted now, perfectly frosted, to match her French manicure and tidy outfit. It all suited her delicate features and petite frame, but made her look more "hands off" than she really was. Or had been. He didn't know, anymore, and didn't want to. He only cared about Karen, who wore her feelings on the sleeve of her loose long sleeve tee, and this entire encounter was torturing her. Time to put a stop to it.

"Sue, you were just heading out, right?" He placed a hand in the small of her back to guide her toward her car, but she resisted. She shot him a quick glance through narrowed eyes and held her ground.

"In a minute."

"Actually, Karen said that there's a whole display of books I could use for my social studies project at the library, she saw it there earlier today, but the kids here are doing the same history projects, hence the display, so if I want a good book, I should go now. We should go now. Okay? Come on." Megan hopped up and down. "Mom, you want to come? I can show you Bun. They make the best hot chocolate ever. Ever. I promise."

He shot Susan a *don't you dare* look, and she had the good grace to not push him further. "Sorry, sweetie, I'm already running late as it is. Good luck with your project, okay?" She tugged Megan into a hug.

With the others temporarily distracted, he turned back to Karen, but he had no words. He cleared his throat and shoved his hands in his back pockets. Was it always going to be this hard? *Until the end of the summer, and then she'll be gone.* The reminder squeezed at this throat. He'd rather be tortured like this than never see her at all. She didn't seem to have the same problem though, because she blinked slowly, almost as if she preferred to not look at him. Fine.

"Meg, I actually have a reference letter to finish writing. You go on to the library with Karen, and we can go for a bike ride when you get back, okay?"

"Dad, come on." She stretched the words out, stopped just short of whining. "I want to go to Bun, too."

He pulled out his wallet and handed her the first bill he found. "Here you go."

Apparently twenty dollars bought a lot of quiet. Meg shut up, and after an awkward wave, Karen was turning around and heading back the way she came, this time with his daughter bouncing alongside. He rubbed his chest, as if that might ease the ache. As if the ache was physical, and not something much harder to heal.

"Want to tell me what that was all about?"

With a start, he realized Susan hadn't left yet. Code white, much? Fuckity fuck. "No."

"I don't think you ever looked at me like that."

There was no malice in her voice, but he didn't need another reminder that he had been a shitty husband. "Don't you have a cottage to get to?"

"Why aren't you together?"

"Susan, seriously, stop."

She stopped, but she didn't leave.

He paced back toward his porch. Her right, to stand on his walk. His right to go inside. Except… "You want to know why we aren't together?" He spun back toward his ex-wife. It wasn't fair, or completely true, but he was pissed and someone was going to hear about it. "Because I spent a month telling myself, and her, that you'd have a problem with it because of Megan. And then when I decided that it was worth it, whatever hassle you were going to give me, then it was too late. She's leaving town at the end of the summer. That's why we aren't together. And it's six different kinds of fucked up, and it's none of your business, so please. Head to your cottage now."

He propped his hands on his hips and hung his head. That was a crapload more than he'd intended to share.

"She's taking our daughter to the library." Susan's voice was low and warm.

"Yeah."

"I wouldn't have a problem with you dating her." He looked up. At least she wasn't pretending she didn't know what he was talking about. An apology was written all over her face. "She's different."

"Yeah."

They exchanged a look that covered the rest of that conversation wordlessly. They weren't friends anymore, just co-parents, and her acceptance of his social life only helped so much. Susan climbed into her car with one last concerned look in his direction.

———

Not his type. She didn't want to believe it, and wouldn't have if he'd said it to anyone else. But now that she'd met Susan, it made sense. Karen had been something different, and there was a base attraction between them that she'd conflated into something special, but was probably more…ordinary for Paul. And since he wasn't looking for a relationship, *not his type* would be easier to compartmentalize.

Unlike Susan, who was the complete package. Pulled together, pretty, hard to resist. She even seemed nice, which made it hard to hate her for touching Paul so much. They touched each other *a lot* for exes that didn't get along. *Didn't they?*

When Paul moved to protect Susan from their conversation, as if Karen might say something to reveal the very little that they'd done together, she expected to be angry. Anticipated white hot rage to flood her veins. But as his arm reached around the petite blond, guiding her toward her car, it was resignation that took up residence in her heart.

Comprehension settled over her like a depressing blanket of mirrors, reflecting back to her all that she wasn't. She was dimly aware of a tiny voice in the back of her head whispering something contrary to the rest of the noise, but by the time they had walked to the library, sorted through the books on display, and hit Bun for hot chocolate, Karen had had enough. She was done, with feeling sad for herself and aching for what might have been with Paul.

As they walked home again, slower this time, savouring the remnants of their hot drinks, Karen introduced Megan to a new term.

"An-acro-nism."

"Close. Not like acrobat, but chronology, like time. Because we're talking about getting things wrong for a time period. Anachronism."

"Wow. That's cool."

"There are some cool books that get creative with it on purpose. I'm going to talk about them at the next reading club, if you want to come. It's on a Saturday morning."

"I'll have to ask my dad. I'd like that, if I'm here." Megan scuffed her foot on the sidewalk. "Karen…"

Don't ask me about your dad. Please don't—

"Why didn't my dad want to come with us today?"

This was a situation that most definitely called for a lie. Ethics be damned. "He had a letter to write. I'm sure he'll come with us next time."

"There will be a next time?" Small and hopeful, Meg's voice cut straight to Karen's heart.

"Yes. Oh, yes." She slid her hand around the girl's smaller hand and squeezed. "I love going to the library with you. I think we just might be kindred spirits when it comes to books."

A small squeeze back told her the feeling was mutual. Another reason to move on and get over her infatuation. There were two people living next door, and Megan could never know about whatever it was that they almost had.

Karen stopped on the sidewalk in front of her house, and shook her head when Megan tugged gently on her hand.

"Awww, come on! I want to show my dad the book you helped me find."

"I bet he's still writing, and I actually have a phone call I need to make." At least that wasn't a complete lie. "Go on by yourself. I'll watch until you're inside. And tell your dad, if he has any questions about reading club, he can text me, okay?"

She added the last bit to reassure Megan that whatever tension she'd picked up between them wasn't going to be a problem. Now she just had to make good on that oblique promise.

10

———

T HE first opportunity to play the cool, unaffected neighbour
came eight days later at the monthly town council meeting.
A rumour had whipped through the community that representatives from national retail chains would be present to discuss leasing options for two store fronts being considered in the community centre plans. Karen was a bundle of nerves after meeting with one of those representatives privately that morning on a separate but related matter. Her parents had entrusted her with the initial discussions on the potential sale of the store, which she mostly resented, when she was being honest about it. But the meeting had gone well, and pretty soon her responsibilities for Wardham Grocery would come to an end, one way or another.

Thankfully, tonight she was just an observer. By the time she arrived at town hall, it was down to standing room only, but as she squeezed in a side door to the council chambers, Evie caught her eye with a furious wave. Her friend was sitting on one of the long benches in the middle of the room, and squeezed over to make space.

"Crazy turn out tonight, eh?" Evie tucked her purse under the seat as Karen joined her.

"Mmm. Any idea who's going to talk tonight?"

"Carrie's speaking about the benefits of letting local companies have first dibs on the space. Dale stopped me on the way in to rant about national chains taking over, which is ridiculous, but I want to support Carrie, and they're sort of on the same side."

Karen rolled her eyes. Only in a deluded way, because Dale was a salesman at the local Ford dealership. Since his very healthy paycheque came from selling an international brand, she didn't get his stake in the issue.

Guilt stabbed through her gut. If Carrie knew what they were considering for the store, two doors down from Bun, she'd probably add it to the agenda tonight. Unlike the community centre, though, there were no public dollars at stake in the decision to sell Wardham Grocery. Her friend might not like it, but it was a private family matter.

But before her thoughts could wind too far in that direction, the crowd shifted and her attention was pulled to a long length of midnight blue against the far wall. Paul stood with Rick Martinez, another constable at the detachment. The younger man was talking quietly in Paul's ear as they surveyed the room, probably giving him the lowdown on everyone in attendance.

Paul had his thumbs notched into the front of his Kevlar vest, a relaxed pose she'd bet a dollar was purposefully adopted. His short sleeved uniform showed off his lean, corded forearms, and she couldn't help but notice the subtle veins and a dusting of hair that gave the topography of his tan skin delicious interest. *That's neither platonic nor aloof.*

She forced her gaze away and did her own assessment of the room. Almost at capacity now. She tried to focus her thoughts on the people around her, but it didn't take long before she was staring at him again. One hand was still tucked into his vest, but the other now worried his bottom lip as he watched the council members file in at the front of the room. She remembered the firm pressure of that lip on hers. The pinch of those fingers on her nipple. How terribly unfair life was that she'd only experienced that through a shirt and bra.

"Karen, stop staring at The Sheriff."

"Stop calling him that." Carrie had coined the nickname and Evie latched on like a kid on a lollipop. Karen exhaled hard and flicked her attention to a hangnail on her thumb. "I'm getting over him."

"I don't believe you."

"Whatever, you don't need to." She pouted for a second, and her friend elbowed her in the side. "No, I really am. Living next door is actually going to make that easier. It turns out he's a bit of a jerk."

She filled Evie in on the overheard conversation that had happened while her friend was out of town, and the blond was halfway out of her chair to give Paul a piece of her mind when the mayor leaned forward and gave a one minute warning into the microphone in front of him. Evie slumped back and glowered across the room. Karen tugged on her arm, desperate to break Evie's magnetic glare at the constables. Paul was far too alert to not feel that buzzing aimed at his head.

"Really, it's for the best. If I thought I was missing out on something special, the summer would drag by. Now I know that the only thing special about Paul was his way with dirty words, and frankly, I've got the internet for that."

Evie giggled, then snorted, her laughter growing instead of fading away as people turned to look at them. Karen couldn't help but join in, and Paul's head jerked in their direction as soon as she guffawed. The ache on his face stole her breath away. He must not have meant to show her anything, because his eyes widened as she paused mid-laugh, and for a second, let her face reflect the same. Bittersweet understanding arced across the room. The noise of the gathering crowd continued around them, but for a moment, they were alone together.

He wasn't perfect. But he was something *a little bit* special. Damn. She needed to work harder at pretending that wasn't the case.

"Seriously, do I need to switch seats with you? Stop looking at him." Evie clapped her hands together twice.

"Shut up. It's not that easy."

"It totally is. I had a one-night stand when I was in Toronto and gave the guy a fake number. You should have done that instead."

"You what???" Of course, the mayor took that moment to raise his hand, and the room magically quieted as Karen's voice rose, so even though she hadn't been yelling, it certainly sounded like it. And everyone was watching them. Karen ducked her head, hand over her face, but at least her friend was laughing beside her. She leaned over and hissed her next words as quietly as she could. "We're acting like teenagers, Evie. This is mortifying."

"Meh. It's fun. I've spent thirty-four years being responsible and boring. Let's live a little. Be bad, get wild."

Karen opened her mouth to point out that it sounded like Evie did more than live *a little,* but people on both sides moved to shush her and she settled for pulling her phone out and typing out a short message to her friend: This isn't over. You'll drive me home?

From the handbag on the floor, Evie's phone dinged with the receipt of said message, and they both shook once again with silent laughter.

Between wanting Paul, which lead to a profound realization that she missed him, and being seriously concerned about her friend's new wild side, Karen barely absorbed any of the town meeting. Carrie spoke at one point, and made a lot of sense, and Dale also got up, but made almost none. She tuned him out and instead focused on the people around her. The vibe of the room was hard to read. Some people were nodding along to all the speakers, but were they just being polite? Others were definitely wary of the representatives from the chains, sitting together in the reserved seats for invited guests at the front. But there was also an undercurrent of annoyance—unless of course she was projecting her own feelings on the crowd, but she didn't think that was the case.

Two rows back, she heard someone shift and cough, and then mutter under their breath, "Don't be selfish, asshole. Jobs are jobs."

Karen didn't know about the proposals for the community centre, but the package she'd been presented that morning about the grocery store would actually mean that her current staff would get a small raise if they sold. It wasn't much, but it was something. She filed that sentiment away in case it was needed in the future. The worry that had gripped her heart for some time eased, just a little.

———

Small town politics would take some getting used to, as would the fact that he was expected to attend town council meetings at all. He respected his detachment commander, though, and Inspector Clark had good reasons for them to share the responsibility of engaging with the community on a rotating basis.

As far as policing needs went, Wardham was a quiet town in a quiet municipality, and their detachment was staffed accordingly. Right now, he and Martinez were at this meeting instead of on traffic duty. Of course, given that the entire adult town population was in this room, they probably wouldn't have any speeding to stop out there.

Whatever. Paul tucked his cynicism away. Why look a gift horse in the mouth? He'd just spent the last hour watching Karen without being a creep. At times during the presentation, she'd looked uncomfortable, shifting in her seat and twisting her hands together, and it hadn't taken him long to figure out that she was worried about how the discussion of public dollars might drift to include her store.

He doubted anyone would care, but if they did, he'd have her back. She might not be speaking to him, but that didn't matter. Nothing mattered if she was upset.

From the periodic gales of laughter that seemed to spontaneously spill out of her and her friend, though, his concern might be premature. Something was bothering her, but it wasn't all consuming. Not yet.

A man drifted toward Rick from the crowd with an extended hand, a booming voice and a slick smile. He raised Paul's hackles immediately.

"Constable Martinez, good to see you again, glad you could come out." As Rick shook the stranger's hand, Paul took in the comfortable leather loafers, quality dress pants and cream golf shirt that expertly disguised a slight paunch. Mr. Slick was about his age, maybe younger, and fancied himself a big fish in this little pond. Whatever his game, Paul wasn't interested in playing.

"Dale, I'd like to introduce Paul Reynolds."

Paul flipped through his mental rolodex. Dale. Ex-husband to Karen's friend, the silly blond with two kids. *How had this guy scored…?* None of his business. "How d'ya do?"

"I'd be better without all this ruckus, but it's good to see something that the town can all band together about." Dale put his hands on his hips and rocked back on his heels. "I tell ya, if we aren't careful, Wardham will turn into another suburb of the city."

Nothing wrong with the city, Paul wanted to point out, but he understood where this man was coming from. His approach was all wrong—his public bluster earlier had lacked finesse, to say the least—but the sentiment of wanting to preserve the small town uniqueness probably started in the right place. "Good that so many people had a chance to say their piece tonight, then."

Dale frowned, like he was parsing Paul's words for hidden meaning. Finding none, he shrugged. "Well, it was nice to meet you. If you're ever in need of a new car, come see me at McCullough Ford. I like to give our boys in blue a good deal."

Rick bit back a laugh at Paul's barely concealed eye roll as the third man drifted away. "Pretty much, man. He's not a bad guy, just…"

"No worries, I get it." Paul wouldn't have given Dale another thought, except he was making a beeline toward Karen. Paul didn't follow, but his muscles twitched, ready to shift into gear if needed. But the salesman pulled up short, and both of them silently observed the woman from the grocery store chain tap Karen on the shoulder and say something perfunctory but pleasant.

It took Paul three seconds to figure out that the women knew each other, and another few beats more to put two and two together. They'd met recently, and in a professional capacity. So far, their discussions had been positive, and both looked forward to talking further. A lot of that was filled in from what he knew of Karen from their previous conversations and his endless capacity to absorb Karen-isms, but some of it would translate to an average observer. The practiced smiles, the handshake. The rep's eagerness. Karen's reluctance to say much of anything.

How much did Dale know about Karen's secret hopes and dreams? Paul tensed and took a step away from the wall and into the room. He'd run interference without a second thought.

She doesn't want to be your problem.

As he often told Megan…tough noogie.

But before he needed to publicly stake a claim on a woman who was pretending to want nothing to do with him, Dale slowly turned and headed for the side door. At least for now, confusion reigned.

11

___

"**Y**OU'VE dodged me long enough."

Evie laughed and moved to the back of the studio space to put away the exercise mats they'd just wiped down and rolled up. All of her Pilates gear lived in a beautiful wood armoire Evie had refinished herself.

"Seriously, Evie, I need to live vicariously through you."

"Still not talking to Paul?"

Karen shook her head. "It's easier this way. Clean break and all that."

"It's never easy. Just different variations on hard." Evie took a deep breath and pulled herself up tall.

"What do you mean? Are you regretting hooking up with that guy?"

"Regret…would be too strong a word. Do you want a drink?" Her friend crossed to the front counter and pulled a pitcher of lemon and mint water from the bar fridge underneath. "It's just… I don't remember the whole night, for one thing, and how terribly irresponsible is that? I'm a mother, for goodness sake. And in order to have that night, I needed to take a train to a city four hours away. Plus, let's not forget that I slept with someone still in college."

Karen choked on her drink. She set the cup down on the counter and waved her hands in the air for a minute before squeaking out her shocked response. "I'm sorry? I'm certainly not going to forget that now, but you did not share that information before."

Evie winced. "Right. I was going to keep that a secret. Stupid, rambling thoughts."

"Was he…legal?"

"Karen Miller, seriously. I was slutty, not evil. He just finished a second degree, so he had to be twenty-three or twenty-four."

"You didn't ask?"

Evie blushed. "We didn't do a ton of talking."

Karen leaned forward. "That sounds lovely. Tell me more."

They both laughed, but before Evie could launch into the naughty details, the door chime rang out. The first few participants for the next class were arriving, so Karen ducked to the back of the studio to grab her bag. Her cell rang as she reached her stuff, and she quickly ducked into the back room. Phones were off-limits, and she didn't want to be banned by Evie.

After convincing her mother that yet another conversation about the pros and cons of selling the store versus hiring a new full-time manager could probably wait until after she'd showered, she shoved her phone deep into her bag—first double checking to make sure it was on vibrate this time.

From the front of the store, a raised male voice drew her attention. The senior citizen brigade weren't the only ones who had joined Evie. Her ex-husband was leaning across the counter, earnestly talking about a sheaf of papers in his hand. Karen wanted nothing to do with Dale, so she hung back, but at the mention of the store, her ears perked up. At the words petition and stop, she was about to charge forward and truly get all "Hulk Smash" on Dale's whiny ass, but as she stepped back into the studio space, she saw her friend hustling Dale the Douche out the door. A quick scan of the counter reassured her that whatever petition Dale was circulating hadn't been left behind.

Evie winced as Karen approached. "You heard?"

"Not everything. Dale's starting a petition about the store?"

"I'm sure it won't get anywhere. He's being an idiot."

"This is my fault for not being totally transparent about the negotiations." Karen felt her shoulders droop, and didn't bother to square them off. She could feel a number of eyes on her, and just didn't care. It wasn't her store, or her problem. She just wanted to be a librarian. "I need a coffee. I need a break from this town, to be honest, but I guess a coffee will have to do."

She waved off Evie's protests. She knew what her friend would say, and she wasn't in the mood to be placated. At this rate, she'd be open to finding a tenant for her house sooner than later and heading to the nearest city at the first opportunity.

The studio was down the street from Bun and her store. *Not* her store anymore. She needed to stop doing that. If no one cared about what was most important in her life, she needed to stop caring about the town and the store and everything else.

People care.

Not enough. Her parents still weren't back. If they cared, they'd come and take these damn negotiations off her plate.

Paul...damn him. Yeah, he cared, too much. And yet still, not enough to get over himself. Not enough to put her first. She had no idea how that could work, but surely it didn't need to be this hard.

Her friends cared, but they had their own shit to deal with. Evie just wasn't political, and saying no to Dale was as much for herself as it was for Karen. Carrie...no way to tell how she'd fall. She certainly had never hesitated to tell Karen when she'd blundered in the past.

She slowed down as Dale trundled out of the new craft store and head into Bun. Damn. Fine, she'd just make coffee at home. Never the same, but whatever.

As she passed the bakery, she couldn't help but glance inside, and instantly regretted the action because Carrie and Dale were standing in the front of the store, right in front of the window.

And Carrie was holding a couple of pieces of paper. Even worse, she was smiling and nodding.

Keep going, Karen urged her feet, but even though her heart couldn't take whatever this was going to be, the rest of her body was curious. She slowed to a stop and watched as Carrie smoothed her hand down Dale's arm and moved to the espresso bar, setting the papers down. Definitely not kicking him out and telling him off.

Bile rose up Karen's throat as she tried to process what she was seeing. *It's something else, Carrie wouldn't...*

Or maybe she would. Karen's feelings weren't sacrosanct. Business, both Carrie's and the town's, mattered.

As if Karen had rung a bell, Carrie's attention snapped to where she was standing on the sidewalk. She held her friend's gaze for a moment, but it hurt too much and gave too little.

Nothing good would come of making a scene. Karen sped home, waiting until she was behind her heavy wood door before letting the tears fall.

She hadn't made it far from that door when, a few hours later, it practically bounced under a quick succession of hard knocks. Too heavy to be Carrie. Sadness unfurled in Karen's chest at the realization that she wanted it to be her friend. That it wasn't. And another emotion twisted inside, as the strength of the knocking forewarned that it might be Paul.

That would be Evie's doing. *Damn her.*

She braced her heart and wrenched open the door. "What are you doing here?"

Instead of answering, he lifted two cups of coffee and stepped inside. He looked good. *Damn him.* And his gazed was filled with far too much understanding. She didn't want the coffee, or his pity.

"I don't want it." She sounded petulant and didn't care.

"Yes, you do."

"Not from Bun I don't."

"Why do you think I'm here?"

That made her pause. "I...I don't know. Evie told you I was upset."

"It was Carrie, actually. She told me about the petition."

"Did she try to get you to sign it?" The words didn't come out easily. She felt brittle and achy, loaded with fear. She didn't really want an answer.

He shook his head and set the coffee down with care. "Come here."

Before she could protest, he'd folded her against his body, tucking her head onto his shoulder. He was wearing a dress shirt, she noticed, as she stared at the pressed collar.

"Why are you dressed up?" she mumbled into his neck.

"Lawyers meeting this morning." His breath was hot against her ear, and she wanted nothing more than to sag into him and let go, but that sounded important.

She eased back, leaving her hands on his shoulders, and looked into his eyes. "Is everything okay?"

He nodded. "Just the usual divorced parent stuff." He placed his hand in the small of her back and steered her into her own living room. "You need to sit."

His voice was firm, but kind, and she thought she might just do anything he said in that moment, as he rubbed a small circle on her back, then slid his hand up to her shoulder and pressed her down to the couch.

"Carrie's not asking people to sign the petition," he said as he retraced his steps to get the coffees. "She was just put on the spot."

"I saw her. She didn't look put on the spot."

"Apparently Dale's considering a run for town council." And so was Carrie. Paul must have learned an awful lot about the politics of their wee town this afternoon.

Karen leaned back against the cushions and closed her eyes. "Oh god, I just had a hissy fit, didn't I?"

Paul chuckled as he joined her on the couch. Even as embarrassment and fear dueled it out throughout most of her mind and body, she was still hyper aware of the heat of his thigh next to hers. The crispness of his shirt sleeve rubbing against the bare of her upper arm. His smell.

"You're wearing cologne."

"I am."

"You don't usually wear any."

"You know that about me?"

She froze on the spot, eyes still closed. But she could feel he was shifting as his arm lifted up and over her head, and without looking at him, she knew he was close. "Uhm. Yeah. You usually smell like soap." She tried to stop there, but her mouth didn't get the message. "And sweat. Not bad sweat, just the nice kind. Fresh, hard working. Honest sweat."

"You just said sweat three times."

She blinked her eyes open. She had to see the smile she heard in his voice, and that was a good call, because it was beautiful. A big curving acceptance of whatever gibberish spilled past her lips, a grin that reached all the way to his eyes.

"It's a good—"

"I get it." He covered her mouth with his in a chaste kiss, his lips just barely feathering over her skin.

She sighed, and slid her hand over the short hair at the back of his head. This was a terrible idea, but she'd missed the feel of him so much. He pressed his lips harder against hers, but when she opened for him and darted her tongue out, part invitation, part tease, he pulled back.

"I need to apologize for what happened when you met Susan."

She really didn't want to talk about that. Ever, but definitely not at that moment. "It's fine."

"It's not even a little bit fine." He rubbed his thumb over her bottom lip. "I've missed you."

Behind her eyelids, hot pressure was building up. "Don't," she whispered. "Just kiss me and let's pretend, just for this afternoon—"

"I don't want to pretend, Karen." His voice was low and soothing, hypnotic. If she wasn't careful, the walls around her heart would crumble before she even noticed. "I...I want to explain."

"No!" She gasped the word. "Please don't." She crawled into his lap and pressed hungry, needy little kisses over his jaw and down his neck as she reached for the buttons on his pressed shirt.

His hands closed over hers and he tugged them into her lap. He choked out her name and tipped his forehead to lean against her chin. "That's not a good idea."

She wanted to weep. It was the first thing that had felt right all day. Longer than that. For weeks, she'd been hollow. He'd given her a taste of being something special, and she wanted that again. She didn't want nice words or kindness. She wanted what she'd never had before. To be irresistible. She wanted to make him want her like she wanted him.

But she was in his lap. She could feel that he did. And even though she knew he would stop her again, she rocked against his erection, and at his stifled groan, she let the tears fall. It shouldn't be this hard. Nothing like tears to turn a guy off, but when she went to scramble off his lap, he held her tight.

"It shouldn't be this hard." This time, the words were whispered out loud. She needed to share the burden in her head, and as he nodded, his cheek rubbing against hers, the pain eased a little.

"I know, darlin'. I wish it were different." His voice was gruff and tight. "But I can't do that."

She nodded blindly as he wiped the tears from her cheek, and after a minute of soaking up his warmth, she eased back to the couch.

"You know this petition isn't going to get any real air, right?

Everyone gets that you need to move on." She glanced up as his voice strained over the last two words. She wished she hadn't. His face was tight and pinched. It made her want things that would never be. Whatever his reasons for staying locked up tight, she wasn't going to sway him. "No one wants to hold you back from your dream."

"What to do with the store...it's not even my decision, you know? I don't know why I'm taking this so personally." She laughed, but even to her own ears it sounded harsh and hollow. "I'm thirty-four, and I want my mommy and daddy to come home and fix my problems."

"They should come home and fix their own problems. They've depended on you for far too long."

————

PAUL LEANED BACK against the couch and stretched out his legs, a deliberate attempt to make himself chill out. He'd stopped at the coffee shop on his way home from the city and interrupted a heated discussion between Karen's friends. As soon as they saw him, the blond one told the redhead that he was the perfect messenger of peace. If he hadn't guessed they were talking about Karen, he would have high-tailed it in the other direction.

Since they were talking about Karen, he pulled up a bar stool.

And now he'd done the opposite of what he'd come here to do. He'd riled her up, and now he was insulting her parents, to whom she was probably inordinately close. He didn't want to think about any of that. He wanted to haul her back onto his lap, strip off her clothes, and feast himself on her body.

But that's what old Paul would do. And he wouldn't think twice about exposing his daughter to a short-term relationship that had no future.

Not anymore. Not even if it killed him.

But Karen didn't know that. From the furtive side glances she kept giving him, it was clear he'd done yet another piss-poor job of explaining himself. *Because now's not the time.* No. His task was to make Karen know she was wanted by the town. Not himself. That would just lead to further confusion and heartache. At this rate, probably his own, the irony of which wasn't lost on him. *Payback's a bitch.*

"I talked to my mom this afternoon. They'll be back in early July."

"Good." Some of his tension seeped away, and he reached out to take her hand. *Friends hold hands.* That wasn't why he wanted to touch her, but it was a reasonable excuse. "What I said before, about missing you. I really have."

She laced her fingers into his and offered a firm squeeze. "Yeah. Me, too."

"If something else like this happens, you text me, okay?"

"Yeah?" Surprise danced across her face.

"What are friends for?" The word stuck in his throat. He coughed. *Man up.* "You deserve to have someone in your corner. And that will always be me, got it?"

"Sure." Her smile was small, but genuine.

He leaned closer, breathing her in, and his chest ached at what was so close and so impossibly off-limits. *If only everything was different.* If only something was different. All it would take is one factor to shift. If she stayed in town. If he could travel more. If Megan was older. If he had more flexibility with Susan. Even after today's meeting, even without the specter of a custody dispute hanging over him, he needed to stay focused.

As easy as it would be to lose himself in her, that wouldn't be fair to either of them. He kissed her on the cheek and pulled back, letting her hand go at the same time. Letting her go, and in the process, finding a way to be close again.

"How about, the next night I have free, we go to Danny's. Hold your head up high and celebrate your new adventure."

"You'd meet me there?" The smile was bigger this time.

"I'd walk you to and from if it guaranteed you'd always be with a friend."

She leaned back and let out a little laughing noise. After all they'd been through, and almost been through, that's what they'd end up being—friends.

It could be worse.

It could be so much better.

12

DALE'S petition was still being circulated, but it had been banned from Danny's, and Bun, and Mrs. Wilkins had started stopping people on the street and telling them to mind their own business about what happened to the store, which was irony of the highest order, but Karen appreciated the support.

The first time she met Paul at Danny's as friends had been hard, but he was there when she arrived, and he walked her home. A few days later, he sent a text message asking if she wanted to meet at Danny's again, this time for trivia night. Again, he walked her home.

It was delicious agony spending time with him in an outwardly platonic way. Inside her head, they were having sex almost constantly, and she was pretty sure he knew that, but they didn't so much as bump elbows when out and about or brush arms on the walks home. No more kisses, however chaste, and no more handholding.

Instead, they talked. About Megan, and Karen's options for school, and Wardham. She gave him tips for the best apple orchards and fall fairs, and they talked about catching up over Thanksgiving. He even helped her put up signs about renting out her house.

She'd mended her relationship with Carrie, but it was Paul who'd surprisingly become the person she turned to first for almost everything in her life. And still they didn't touch. They didn't dare, as if they both knew their friendship was too precarious to survive temptation.

The terms of their new relationship seemed generous with respect to time of day. She'd woken up early one morning, only to have her cell phone go off five minutes later. Paul had just arrived home from a night shift and noticed her light on. They talked for a few minutes before he went to bed, but it was enough of a precedent that when she came home from a trip to Toronto one night in late June, and his light was on, she thought about knocking on his door.

But they hadn't crossed that boundary again. Hadn't spent time together in either of their homes. Like they both knew that would be asking too much.

So instead she pulled out her phone. He picked up right away, and she smiled at his warm greeting.

"I just got back. It went well. I found a couple of apartment options and visited the school. Did some shopping, had sushi for dinner." She opened her car door, pausing for a moment to give Hermoine a loving pat. They'd avoided rush hour neatly, and the drive home had been fun. Lee Brice on the stereo, windows down…she wouldn't mind being in the city if all trips home were that easy. It would be hard in the winter, but it would be worth it to see—

She froze beside her car as the realization that she was still hung up on Paul slammed into her chest. Crap on a stick. Yes, he still fueled her fantasies, but that's all they were. All they could be. She wasn't going to come home to see him. Her family, sure. But she'd never have that thought about Carrie or Evie.

"Karen?" He'd been talking in her ear, but it wasn't until he repeated her name that she tuned back in.

"I'm sorry, I was just thinking about—I have to go." She hung up, but that didn't stop him from opening his back door.

He stood there in a black t-shirt and faded blue jeans, barefoot and backlit by his kitchen, and she waved. What else could she do?

"What's going on?" He flicked the light off and closed up his house before jogging down the stairs toward her. "You okay?"

"I'm fine, I'm sorry, it's just been a long day. I'm going to go inside."

He grinned and gestured at her heels. "Right, you hate the fancy clothes."

At the reminder of what happened the last time she had put on, and then taken off, a skirt and blouse, she flushed and turned. "Night, Paul."

"I didn't mean…ah crap, Karen, I'm sorry." She climbed the steps to her back deck before pausing. But she didn't turn around. She didn't know what she might say or do if she did. His footsteps were light and cautious. She felt him stop not far behind her. "I'm going to put my foot in my mouth sometimes."

"I'm not offended," she whispered.

"Then don't run away. I'll grab some beers, we can sit on the deck and you can tell me more about shopping."

She let out a laugh despite herself and did a quarter turn to glance at him. "You want to hear about shopping?"

He shrugged. "I like spending time with you."

She turned around fully, and opened her mouth to accept his offer, when his gaze dropped to her chest. It was just for a second before he glanced down and away, but it was enough.

"You know what? I have a better idea." She stepped toward him and pressed her palms to his hard chest. Oh god, the feel of him under her skin. She'd never get enough of that, but one night would have to do. "I think we should talk more about the last time I wore a skirt. I think we should do more than talk about it."

He drew in a ragged breath and brought his hands up to hers. "That's not a good idea."

"And yet you aren't pushing me away." She forced her voice to stay light. Hopefully inviting, and not needy. She wasn't begging for anything, but she wanted to get this pulsing desire out of her system.

"Because I'm not a good man, Karen." He squeezed her wrists, then stroked his hands up her arms.

"You're a cop."

"One doesn't have anything to do with the other."

"You're a good man."

"I wasn't a good husband."

"I'm not looking for a husband."

"I'm not a good boyfriend."

She took a step back. "I'm not sure why we're having this conversation then."

————

He swallowed hard. It was what he wanted, but pushing her away still felt like a sucker punch to the gut. "Exactl—"

"—because," she continued, trailing her fingers up her middle until she was toying with the top button on her shirt. "I'm not looking for anything beyond tonight."

Darkness had descended, but they were still outside. And she was, one button at a time, revealing a strip of skin bisected by a black lace bra. He couldn't tear his eyes back to her face for anything in the world. And didn't that just prove his point? So he closed them instead. "You should be."

"Why?"

He couldn't exactly say. He blinked in surprise, refocusing his gaze on her face. "Because you deserve a good man."

That was the wrong answer, clearly, because her fingers flew back up the front of her blouse, cutting off the previously extended invitation. Modesty restored, Karen settled her hands on her hips and pinned him in place with a blazing stare.

"Really." She bit out the words. "Tell me more about how my life is empty without a *good man*."

When she put it like that, it didn't sound quite right. "That's not..."

"Yes, it is. You said it. Own it."

He scrubbed his hand over his face and up into his hair. "Damn. I'm just trying to do the right thing here. I don't want to hurt you."

Her face softened, but her posture didn't change. She was tough, even when she liked him. Which was more often than he deserved. "Do you think that I can't protect myself? That one night with you will forever ruin me for other men?"

He winced. He hoped she'd misread his expression as contrition, an acknowledgement that he was a buffoon, but he was dumb and she was smart, so there was little chance of that happening.

"Because that's what you just suggested." Her voice dropped a register as she shifted closer. "Instead of inviting you in tonight to do...things, you think I should find someone else to warm my bed. Permanently. Someone nice. *A good man—*"

He hauled her hard against his body, driving one hand into her hair as the other wrapped tightly around her waist. "Enough," he rasped. "Stop."

She shook her head slowly, her gaze never leaving his. "No. You don't get to push me away without acknowledging what that means."

"So that wasn't your principles talking? You just wanted to goad me into losing control?" He slanted his face just above hers. "Because I can do that. But neither of us is going to like me much in the morning."

"I don't like you much right now," she whispered, but her face was still soft.

He cursed under his breath. "And I like you too much for my own good."

She laughed softly and arched in his arms. "One night, Paul. Let's get this tension between us out of our systems. Nothing will change. I'm still moving to Toronto. We'll still be friends. But I won't always be wondering…"

She trailed off, and he growled. No way was she leaving that left unsaid. "Wondering what, darlin'?"

He loved the way she blushed. "Uhm." She sucked in a breath, and let the next words spill out in a lusty pile. "If you're as good in person as you are on the phone."

That was a challenge he was more than up for. He nudged their faces together, savouring their first kiss in almost a month with tender reverence. If they only had tonight, he was taking the whole night. There was no need to rush. Except Karen wasn't on board with that plan, and as she slid her hands under his t-shirt and up his bare back, he knew he needed to move them inside.

"Do you have condoms?" he asked against her mouth.

"Mmm-hmmm. I picked up one at the health fair last week."

He laughed hard, wrapping his arms tighter around her as she squirmed in protest.

"What's so funny about that?"

He pulled her away from her door and toward the steps. "Come on, darlin'. We'll take this to my place. First of all, you've been thinking about this for a week—"

"I have not!"

"Part of you has, clearly." He stopped in their driveway to kiss her quickly, pulling their hips together. Karen moaned into his mouth, and he nipped her lip. "And secondly, one condom isn't going to cut it."

She hissed softly and he lightly slapped her ass. "Intrigued? Get inside."

She practically ran up his steps, and since he hadn't locked his door, was already in his kitchen when he reached her. "You have a nice place."

"Thanks." He nudged her from behind, and she took a deep breath as he wrapped one arm around her waist, holding her tight against his hard-on, and used the other to sweep her hair away from her neck so he could press his mouth to the juncture where it met her shoulder. He was going to enjoy discovering what made her gasp and what made her shiver. If she liked teeth, or tongue, or both.

He inhaled the scent of her skin. The faintest hint of something tropical, worn away by a long day, leaving just her. Soft and sweet and warm.

He'd almost convinced himself that this was never going to happen. A missed opportunity that he'd always wonder about. Karen, the one who got away. But tonight, she was right here, in his arms.

"Is your bedroom upstairs?" She gasped as his fingers worked the buttons at the front of her shirt.

"Mmmm. Yes. But I don't think we'll get there for a little bit yet." He turned her around and kissed her again. Tonight was a gift, and he was going to give as much as he could right back. And not just her passion. She was also giving him her trust. That they could do this and go back to being friends tomorrow. He'd make sure that happened. He wasn't going to mope over what couldn't be. One night would never be enough, but it was all they had.

He reached down her hips and gathered the material of her skirt in his hands, slowly bunching it higher and higher until his fingertips met soft, bare skin. That simple touch, his fingers on her thighs, was sweeter and hotter than he'd imagined it would be, and without thinking about it, he deepened the kiss. His tongued stroked hard against hers, a promise of what was to come. His mouth on her pussy. His cock inside her. Stroking her to orgasm after orgasm, until she collapsed bonelessly in his bed.

She wrapped her arms around his neck and met him stroke for stroke, and the taste of her eagerness was better than anything else he'd ever experienced. He nudged her back against his kitchen table, and after cupping her sweet ass in his palms for a moment, carefully sat her on the edge.

He broke off their kiss and looked down at the space between their bodies. Her skirt was rucked up around her waist, her blouse half undone, and his erection proudly strained against his fly. "This time, darlin', I want to see it when you spread your legs for me."

She leaned her forehead against his and inched her long thighs apart. Tonight her underwear was black cotton, and her soft skin looked deliciously pale in comparison. He was breathing as hard as she was as he trailed one hand north from her knee. She hadn't shaved here, and as his fingers drifted over the sparse, fine hairs, she tensed.

"You're beautiful," he whispered. "I don't want to wait until we go upstairs, can I touch you now?"

"Can you?" She let out a reedy breath. "You better."

"I've thought about you like this so many times."

"Tell me about that." Her words slipped out on a whisper.

He stepped closer, pushing his hips between her knees. "You want to hear about me fisting my cock in the shower, thinking about you writhing around on your bed?"

Her eyes dilated and she sucked her lower lip into her mouth for a second before releasing it with a wet pop. "Yes."

"Sometimes I wake up in the middle of the night, so sure that you've got your hand wrapped around me. That you're stroking me."

She dropped one hand from around his neck and dragged it down his torso to his jeans, desperate to have the proof of how much he wanted her under her fingers. His cock flexed against her touch, and he groaned. "Just like that, but skin-on-skin. So hot."

He stopped her as she went for the button. "Not yet. Soon. First I want to touch you. Lick you." He leaned closer and whispered in her ear. "Taste you."

Her legs squeezed tight on his hips and she shivered. He stroked his thumb lightly over her core, noting with the puffed ego of a peacock that she was soft and wet beneath the cotton, and he would return there momentarily. But first, he wanted to see and feel the breasts that had been tantalizing him for months, bouncing joyfully in front of him when she was strictly hands-off. He brought his attention north to her blouse, which was pretty but needed to disappear. He slid it off, not wanting to let his brute loose just yet, then shifted his body weight, pressing Karen back until she dropped her hands to brace herself on the table. He sucked her lower lip into his mouth for a second, then trailed his mouth down her jaw and onto her neck, tipping her head back as he reached first into one bra cup, and then the other, lifting and freeing her breasts.

Twin swells, and an intoxicating valley between them. He didn't know where to go first, so he blazed a quick trail of attention from left to right with his tongue, dipping in the middle, before pulling back for a moment to appreciate how tight and dark her nipples went when turned on.

"Seriously beautiful," he muttered under his breath, but she heard him and he was glad. He latched on to the right nipple with a wide, hungry mouth, desperate to suck on her, make that pebbled flesh swell and bloom in his mouth. At the first gentle tug of suction, she squeezed her legs tighter around his hips, pulling their cores together. At the second ministration, she rocked against him, and he lifted his left hand to her other breast, teasing first the flesh and then the nipple itself with light, feathery strokes. Each touch wound her legs tighter. Each suck elicited an excited gasp and a grind against his cock.

She might get off like this.

Hell, he might get off like this.

When was the last time he came in his pants like a fifteen year old? Probably when he was fifteen. Jesus.

With a pop, he switched sides, matching the strokes of his tongue and the roll of her now puffy and pliable nipple with the increasing rhythm of their hips. The table jerked hard against the wall as she ground tight circles against his jeans, and he rocked faster against her, wanting her to get there before he was past the point of no return.

She wrenched one of her hands off the table and wrapped it

around his head, holding him to her breast as she arched one final time and seized against his body, holding still for a moment before tremors took over. He eased both arms around her back and trailed his mouth back to hers, pressing sweet, wet kisses to her pulse points on the way.

Her hair was wild and damp, her eyes bright and dark at the same time, and she looked magnificent. He told her as much, over and over again, as he swept her into his arms, ignoring her protests. She wasn't light, but he could carry her easily. Hell, he'd carry her if it wasn't easy. He'd walk over burning coals to make sure that she was worshiped appropriately. She was a goddess, and his adoration was just beginning.

13

A T the top of the stairs, Paul strode into the first bedroom and placed her on a large, elevated bed. Dimly lit, with just the hall light spilling in, shadows filled most of the room, which she was fine with—now that she was coming down from her orgasm, she was a bit embarrassed about what just happened in his kitchen. His bright, for-eating in, kitchen. *Oh god.* She covered her face with her hands and groaned.

"Oh, no. No, no, no, no, no." She peeked through her fingers. Paul had paused mid-strip to mock-glower at her. "Bring back the brazen hussy who propositioned me outside. I'm not done with her yet."

"I have no idea who that woman is," she whispered. *But I think I like her.*

He stalked toward the bed, still in his briefs. He was wiry and tight, everywhere, and the light from the hall bounced off the sharp angles of his body, exaggerating the shadowy ridge running down the center of his six-pack. Her hands fell away from her face and she shrugged off the nerves. The jut of his erection promised she didn't have to waste second thoughts on anything they'd done, or would do.

"Aren't you going to, uhm, take those off?" She ached to see all of him, need burning in every cell of her body. And, despite her post-orgasmic nervous reaction, she wanted to be naked too, and finally have nothing between them.

"Soon." He climbed onto the bed and covered her body with his, holding himself up on his forearms. "That was really awesome, downstairs." He bent his head and pressed his mouth close to her ear. "I almost came in my pants."

She felt his grin against her cheek before he pulled back and she saw it, his teeth bright in his face as he shook with laughter. And she couldn't do anything but join him, because that was pretty funny. "Seriously?"

He nodded. "You felt unreal, grinding against me like that. I probably should have done math or something."

"You didn't?"

"Couldn't. There was no room in my head for thought, let alone complex equations."

A hot flush tingled through her as she beamed. So this was what it felt like to be a vixen. Awesome. "Wow. I had no idea."

He wove his fingers through hers and stretched their arms high and wide, sinking the weight of his upper body carefully onto her as he pressed his open mouth to her neck.

"Paul." She moaned his name more than once, repeating it again and again as he stoked her desire, building the heat in her core from the coals of his last efforts. She twisted and arched her body against his, presenting new patches of skin for him to nip and lick and lave, until his mouth met hers and they lost themselves in a desperate, all-consuming kiss to end all kisses.

He released her hands and shifted his legs, moving enough to divest them both of their clothes, and she stroked his jaw, then the cords in his neck, and his tight, round shoulders, the muscles bunching and shifting under her hands as he jerked her skirt down her hips, his mouth still feverishly consuming her lips. Her tongue. Her breath.

His knees pressed her thighs apart, and this time she didn't hesitate to open as wide as possible for him.

When his fingers found her wet core, she groaned and lifted her hips, begging for any part of him to be inside her. He obliged, slicking first one, then two digits into her pussy, then up and through her folds to her clit before dipping in again. He stroked, deep and smooth, turning his fingers a bit each time, pressing inside her in the most delicious ways.

His cock bobbed against her thigh, as if asking for attention, and she reached through the tangle of their pressed together bodies, wanting to touch it. She wanted more than that—she wanted to see it, lick it, consume it…worship it. As her left hand found him, rock hard and silky smooth, ridged in all the right places, she shivered, and Paul paused, his fingers just grazing her sex.

"What is it?"

She shook her head. "Don't stop."

He lifted his hips, giving them both more room to move their hands and fingers as they resumed pleasuring each other. The combination of his finding all of her secret buttons, and the hard, hot length of him in her hand, finally, was too much, in the very best way possible. She slammed her thighs shut, pinning his hand in place as she rocked over the cliff of another orgasm, unexpectedly finding herself in free fall.

Paul slid to his side, best as he could with his hand caught between her legs, and she rolled toward him, like a blind kitten seeking the warmth of its mother. She jerked as he slid his hand free, whimpering slightly as he accidentally touched her engorged clit. "Sorry, darlin'," he whispered, stroking her hip. "That was beautiful, too. I could…"

There was no need for him to finish the sentence. However much they might both want to do that again and again, they only had tonight. Any other time, with any other person, Karen would have thought two orgasms were plenty, and be kind of meh on the idea of doing anything else. She was verging on sore, already, but they were going to make this one night count. The memory of it was going to need to last a long time. *Forever.* She swallowed that thought, pushing it out of her mind. All that mattered was the here and now. And Paul still hadn't come.

"Can I ask you a delicate question?" She shifted onto one arm, deliberately letting her nipples trail against his torso. Vixen-esque. She giggled, and he raised an eyebrow. "No, ignore that. Post-orgasm laugh, nothing to do with the question." She cleared her throat and drifted the palm of her hand down the trail of fuzz running south from his navel. "How many times…"

The question died in her throat as her hand connected with his cock. The feel of him against her palm actually made her a little dizzy. She stroked him a few times, enjoying the grunts and groans he made as he pressed his head back against the pillow, and pouted when his hand came around hers and stilled her action.

"Finish your question," he growled, and she blushed. "I think I know what you're asking, but I want to hear the words come out of your pretty mouth."

"How many times can you come?"

He growled again, and encouraged her to resume the handjob. "Why?"

"Because…" She trailed off again, but given the way he was jerking his hips and moaning, there was no reason to be embarrassed about a few words. Or probably anything. "I'd really like for you to come in my mouth."

Paul pushed himself up and shifted faster than Karen would have thought humanly possible, bringing his cock closer to her face. She leaned forward and pressed a delicate kiss to the velvety soft head. This angle wasn't going to work, although the thought of lying back and letting Paul fuck her face gave her an intense and unexpected thrill. Right now, though, she wanted to give as much as she had received. She swiped a bead of pre-come with her tongue, and giggled as he groaned. She could feel his hands waving in the air on either side of her head, and that idea pleased her too. *Yes, grab my hair. Push your cock into my mouth.* How could one night be enough when there were literally dozens of ways she wanted to give him a blowjob?

She crawled onto her hands and knees, settling in front of Paul. He reached out and squeezed her shoulders, then softened his hands, leaving them on her skin. In the dim light and quiet of his bedroom, she was struck by the special intimacy of this act. She opened her mouth and felt the heavy tip of him rest on her tongue. She could smell soap on the rest of his body, but his cock just tasted manly—clean, with a hint of salty musk. Enough to cloud her senses and trigger a base hunger for more.

His hips swayed, not pressing exactly, but enough to remind her that he hadn't come yet. She relaxed her throat and rocked forward, enjoying the slide of his shaft into her mouth, then out again. She savoured the noises he made as she swirled her tongue around and underneath the velvet head. As she pressed firmly around his girth with her lips and hummed.

Carefully balancing on one hand, she brought the other up between his legs, loving the coarse rub of the hair on his thighs, and then his sharp moan as her fingers circled his scrotum before joining her mouth, adding an opposite stroke to her swirling tongue. Again and again, her fist and her mouth moved together and apart, twisting delicately to meet in the middle of his cock. His hips started to jerk as well, and his vocalizations promised she was doing something right, so she kept it up as he swelled harder still, then exploded, spilling himself on her tongue.

He continued to rock into her mouth gently as she swallowed, even as his legs shook and his torso curved over her head, his arms alternately stroking and tapping helplessly against her back. When his cock stopped twitching, he eased back and slumped against the headboard, pulling her into his side.

"I think I blacked out there for a minute." His voice was hoarse, and she smiled.

"I'm going to take that as a compliment." She licked her lips. She could still taste him. She should probably—

"What's going on in your head?" His eyes were still closed,

but his arm had turned into a band of steel, holding her firm against him.

"I was just thinking I'd go and rinse my mouth out."

"For you, or for me?" He blinked one eye open and gave her a big, lazy grin. "Because if it's for me, I'd rather keep your naked body pressed up against mine. After a blowjob like that, I don't care what your mouth tastes like."

"Uhm…" Okay, then. It certainly wasn't for her. She liked the smell of his sweat. She was cool with the taste of his come.

"Come here." He dragged her onto his chest. They were almost the same height, and he wasn't huge. How did he move her around so effortlessly? He pressed his lips to hers, then traced the seam of her lips with his tongue. She opened for him with a sigh, and he proved that it really wasn't an issue. "Are you sleepy?"

"No." She really wasn't. She'd spent the night before in the city, so she'd actually slept in a little. Her stomach growled, loud in the silence. "I might be hungry, though."

He kissed her again before rolling her onto her back. "You definitely deserve a sandwich, come with me."

She looked at her crumbled skirt and blouse, and laughed in relief when he tossed her his t-shirt instead. She pulled it on, secretly pleased that it fit, hitting the top of her thighs in what she hoped was a sexy way. He copped a feel of her ass as he padded past her to grab his jeans, so she was guessing it was good enough for him. And his wardrobe choice most definitely worked for her —his jeans left unbuttoned, chest bare, he was effortlessly sexy, and if her stomach hadn't taken that moment to growl, she'd have pulled him back to bed.

He jogged down the stairs, giving her good hope for his recovery in other ways, and by the time she found him in the kitchen he'd pulled out whole grain sandwich loaf, tomatoes, lettuce, mayonnaise and a block of cheese.

"Anything you don't like?" He tossed the question at her over his shoulder as he efficiently sliced and spread. She answered in the negative, and looked around for something to do. She didn't even know where to look for glasses, but he probably had beer in the fridge.

She was right. "Want one?"

He nodded, and she popped the caps off two bottles, bringing them to the table as he plated up their sandwiches. Her cheeks pinked at their recent activity in this very spot—two of the three chairs still shoved out of the way.

Paul bumped her hip with his as he set their plates on the table, then turned and pulled her into his arms. "I didn't think this was ever going to happen," he said, his voice low and intense. "I know we're at different places in our lives, but I want you to know that this is special for me."

She didn't know how to respond to that. She understood what he was—and wasn't—saying. And it was fine. Of course she'd want more than him. He'd already done the marriage and kids thing, and come out the other side with a cynicism she'd never understand. But he'd wanted more than a single night. On that front, they were at the same bittersweet place. And it was there that she found the right words to keep them on track.

"Our chemistry is real, and unique. I've never...tonight has never happened with anyone else for me. Not like this. But maybe it's special in part because we're going in opposite directions." She pressed a finger against his lips as they parted in protest. "No, don't. There's no point in wishing things were different when they can't be, right?"

The set of his jaw said he didn't agree with something she said, but his eyes were gentle and after a beat, he kissed her and pressed her into one of the chairs. "Come on, let's eat." He leaned over and brushed his lips past her ear. "You're going to need your strength tonight."

And just like that, the momentary awkwardness passed. The sandwiches and beer went down quickly, and before long Paul was checking the locks at the front and back door and turning off lights. Something about his maneuvers told Karen she was spending the whole night, and the thought thrilled her. Would one night together include morning sex? Maybe she'd wake him up with another blowjob.

"Whatever you're thinking about right now, I like it." He held out his hand and led her to the stairs. "Brave enough to share?"

She laughed quietly and took his direction to lead the way. "I was thinking about how much I enjoyed everything I had in my mouth tonight."

Silence wasn't the response she expected, so she stopped and turned back to look at him. The blast of heat in his gaze made her insides melt in anticipation. Her breath hitched as he moved up the two steps between them, stopping immediately below her. His hands met her bare legs at the knee, and ghosted north until his grip tightened at the top of her thighs, his fingers curling around the front, his thumbs teasing the curve of skin where her legs met her bottom.

"I knew you were going to be trouble," he muttered, squeezing her flesh. "How the fuck am I going to get those words out of my head after tonight?"

Her gut clenched. So they'd both have vivid fantasy material. It was only fair. And he kept filling those coffers with responses like that. She'd never forget the press of his fingertips sinking into her legs. Knowing that her ass and pussy were right there, bare and accessible, and it was just *her* that he wanted to hold on to for a moment while he wrestled for control. Knowing that it wouldn't be long before he shifted his attention to the aforementioned bits, and that would be awesome, too.

She turned, slowly, and took his hands. Without breaking eye contact, she moved backwards up the stairs, guiding her lover back to bed. In his room, she peeled off his t-shirt and stood naked. He raised his hands to her face, kissing her gently at first, then harder and deeper until they were both breathless.

"Can I turn the light on?" he asked, his voice rough with need. She nodded silently, and he eased her back onto the bed, kissing her again on the mouth before moving south to love her breasts, then the softness of her middle, her hips, and finally her very core. He pressed his face into her curls, then stroked her thighs, guiding them up and apart.

"Fuck, yes," he muttered, as she slid one ankle up and over his shoulder. "Wrap the other one around, too."

She did as she was told, her face hot with equal parts anticipation and anxiety. She was soaking wet, and spread wide open. And she wanted his mouth on her so much it hurt. That need trumped everything else.

"Paul…" she keened his name, and he roughly slid his hands under her ass, tilting her pelvis up at the same time as his mouth descended.

This was a kiss unlike any other.

His whole mouth covered her pussy as his tongued explored her for the first time, licking between her folds and around her clit, then searching out her entrance and delving deep, lapping up everything she gave him and demanding more. He growled as she surged against his face, squeezing her skin hard enough that he might leave marks. She arched her back, trying to get him to hold on even harder. He snaked one arm under and around her hip, placing it flat against her stomach, pinning her in place as he sucked her clit into his mouth, pulling and licking at the same time. He was driving her insane.

"Fuck me." The words tore out of her mouth on a wail, and she repeated them twice more, thrashing her head from side to side. In a flash, he was on top of her, his cock hard against his hip, and he was reaching past her toward the bedside table. With a crash, he wrenched the drawer open and dragged a strip of condoms onto the bed beside them. He ripped open the foil blindly as he kissed her. Her scent covered his face. She wanted him to do that again and again. Panic rose from her chest into her throat, and she pushed it away. "Paul, I need you inside me."

"I know, baby."

Fuck. Where did that name come from? And why did it make her want to cry?

He paused above her. "You still with me?"

"Oh god, yes." Even if it broke her, she needed this.

"I need you, too."

She gasped as he sank into her, filling her completely, pushing the ache and fear away. He paused there, his hips seated fully against her bottom, and buried his face in her neck. She wrapped her limbs around his body, wanting to freeze the moment just as much as he did. But she was also on the brink, having been driven precariously close to the edge by the first thrust, and her body craved that release even if her mind wasn't ready to let go just yet. As if her core had a mind of its own, her pelvis rocked against his, grinding her clit against the base of his cock, eliciting a groan in return.

Against her neck, he opened his mouth, sucking a bit of her skin into his mouth as he eased his hips back, then nipping gently as he surged into her again. She gasped, and he pulled her knees higher, shifting his entry to stroke a different part of her. A groan tore out of her chest, and he wrapped one hand around her neck, pulling their faces together.

"Tonight, you're mine."

"I'm yours," she whispered, hot tears pricking at her eyes as her orgasm loomed fierce around them.

"Never doubt that this is real." He ground out the words as he pressed his other hand against the headboard and let himself go, driving his hips home hard and fast, over and over again until they both exploded in bittersweet release, their mind-blowing pleasure tinged with the agonizing knowledge that dawn would soon arrive.

14

———

H E gave her a goddamn hickey.

She grinned at her reflection in the bathroom mirror, and went in search of a muslin scarf. Totally worth it, but difficult to cover up in the summer heat.

Paul had been right. They'd needed two more condoms that night, each of them taking turns waking the other before dawn finally arrived.

Sleeping with him had been an unexpected pleasure in itself. His body, hard and taut with tension while conscious, softened to a warm, snuggly blanket as he slept. Which he somehow did both under and on top of her—pulling her over his torso, then sliding one arm around to rest across her back and notching one leg onto her hip.

Waking up had been bittersweet and deliberately PG-13. Neither had known quite what to say, so they silently showered, made and drank coffee, and got dressed, all without talking. They exchanged a few words, but not the important ones. Not the decisive ones. About if they could stick to the one-night plan, when they both wanted more. Or if they might be brave and take a leap into the unknown, knowing it wasn't ideal, but since it was all they could have, why not have it while they could?

Why not?

The question rolled over in her head as she changed again at home. She twisted the possible answers in every conceivable direction as she checked email, watered plants, put on laundry and by the time her phone rang mid-morning, she was quite certain there was no barrier that couldn't be overcome. So she answered with more gaiety than she'd felt in a month, but her mood quickly evaporated as her mother's teary words spilled out of the handset.

"Slow down, Mom, I can't understand what you're saying." She swallowed hard against the panic rising in her chest. "Who's in the hospital? Where are you?"

"Saint uhm…St. Louis. It's your brother." The words fell away, overcome by shaking and sobbing, and in the background, her dad's voice got louder as he took the phone.

"Karen, Chad's been in an accident." Her father never called Chase by his given name. *Oh god.* "He was hit by someone who ran a red light. He's in surgery right now, but we should know more soon."

"Dad?" She couldn't ask what she really wanted to know. It didn't matter as much as his life.

"It's his legs, sweetie."

No. A keening wail threatened to rip out of her chest and she stuffed her fist in her mouth. A thousand kilometers away, her mother made a matching sound, and Karen's heart broke. All of their hopes and dreams for their oldest son… "Do you need me there?"

"I don't know. I'll call Davis next, can you call Audrey?"

"I can call both of them."

Her dad sucked in a shaky breath. "Okay. Thank you. We'll be heading back into the hospital in a second, so we'll need to turn our phones off, but we have our laptop and I think there's wi-fi."

Karen took down the hospital details and promised to email shortly. Then she dialed her younger brother and willed herself not to lose it.

"Yo, sis, what's up?" Music and crackling loudspeaker announcements surrounded Davis's voice.

She took a deep breath. "Can you go somewhere quiet?"

"Sure, hang on a sec." The noise muffled for a moment, then she heard shuffling and the click of a door. "What's going on?"

She never called him. Their communication was limited to text messages, mostly dirty jokes and pokey reminders not to forget about family birthdays. "It's Chase."

"Shit, what happened? What do I need to do?" That was the Miller way. Leap to action.

"He's been...Mom and Dad are with him, but Davis...he's been in a car accident. He's in surgery."

"Where?"

"St. Louis. I'm going to call Audrey next, I think we could probably get a direct flight there this afternoon from Detroit."

"I'm in San Diego. I doubt there's a direct flight, but I'll see what I can do." He tightened his voice, probably fighting for the same control she desperately needed. They both wanted to do something. Doing might put their panicky adrenaline to good use. "What kind of surgery?"

It took two false starts to force the words out. "I think his legs were injured in the crash. Dad didn't say, exactly. He probably doesn't know yet."

"Fuck!" A loud crash told her Davis had kicked or thrown something across the room. "Does the media know yet?"

Oh, crap. "I have no idea. I hadn't thought about..."

"I'll call his agent. When you get to the hospital, try and find a side entrance."

"No one will know who we..."

"Just in case."

"Okay."

"Kar...what was he doing there?"

That was the million dollar question. Chase had given their parents tickets to Game Six of the Stanley Cup series, but after his own team had been eliminated earlier in the playoffs, Karen didn't expect her brother to go to the game with them. So what had he been doing in St. Louis? "I don't know."

"Okay. You're alright to drive?"

No. "Yes."

"Be safe."

"Yeah."

"I'll see you later tonight or tomorrow."

The next call was even harder. Audrey was out for a late diner breakfast with some friends, and started crying right away. She passed the phone to a friend, who promised Karen she'd get her baby sister back to the dorm and pack her an overnight bag.

After doing the same for herself, Karen called Melody and asked her work an extra shift, and call the rest of her staff and let them know she was going to be out of town for a couple of days. Melody didn't ask why, and Karen didn't offer, but by the time she was standing on her deck, locking her back door, a text message had come in from Davis. Someone from the team and Chase's agent were en route to the hospital, since they were already in St. Louis, and given how much media presence there was in the city for the series finale, the accident would probably be breaking news before they got on the plane.

She pushed furious tears off her cheeks. That was the last thing her family needed.

"Karen?" She lifted her head in surprise. Paul was moving across the driveway in her direction, worry etched on his face. "What's wrong?"

"My brother." She gulped for air. "He's been in a car accident in the States."

"What do you need?"

"Uhm…" Her mind was blank. She shook her head, desperate to focus. "I'm going. I need to pick up my sister in Windsor, then we'll go to the airport in Detroit and fly to St. Louis."

"Do you have tickets?"

"Not yet. I was going to do something about that when I got to Windsor and had Audrey with me."

He flashed a glance at his watch and pulled out his phone. "Come on, I'll drive you."

"It's okay." She hated how small and pathetic her voice sounded. She was tough. She could do this on her own.

He stopped typing for a second and looked at her like she was an idiot. Except with a bit of affection, which she appreciated. "It's not okay. Your brother…which one?"

"Chase."

Understanding flashed across Paul's face. He could see the massive impact that she couldn't yet fully comprehend. "Something awful has just happened to your entire family. It's not okay, and I can't do much, but I can do this." He pulled her hard against his body and smoothed his hand over her hair, pressing her face into his neck. "I'll drive you and your sister to the airport."

"Okay." She whispered the word against his skin. Behind her back, he started tapping away at his phone again, and she let the clickety clack from his Blackberry keyboard drift into her head and push away the panic. Whatever he was doing, it was more than she was capable of right then.

A wave of fresh panic swelled from deep in her gut, and before the silent cry turned into something else, Paul had tightened his arms around her and brought his mouth to her ear. "We just need to get to Windsor, baby. Focus on that. Twenty minutes from now, you'll have your sister to take care of. You going to be able to do that?"

She nodded. Somehow, she'd find the strength.

He led her to his garage, where he stowed her bag in the trunk. Déjà vu washed over her, the action triggering a recollection of their first conversation. She'd never have imagined that he'd be such a good friend. He'd seemed so solitary, barely aware that he was living in a community at all. Oblivious to her, and his place in her life. Or at least, his car's place in her driveway.

But now…he still had no idea how much she'd come to need him. How much she wanted him, that was no secret. But outside of their chemical reaction…this man had become her best friend. And in two short months, she'd be far away. If something happened—when something happened, because *fuck*, life was just like that, wasn't it?—Paul wouldn't see her out his window. Wouldn't be next door to drive her to the airport. Wouldn't—

The press of his hand at the small of her back jerked her attention back to the task at hand. He murmured something about getting his passport, and then he stepped back. She nodded dumbly and slid into the car. It was tidy, just like everything else in his life. Like his life itself. Except for her, the trouble he didn't want and couldn't resist. After he returned and pulled out of the garage, she closed her eyes and tilted her face toward the side window. She couldn't go there right now, but she couldn't hold herself back, either.

"Thank you." She cleared her throat. "Do you have time to do this today?"

Low and immediate, his response warmed her core and sparked bits of hope she didn't want to latch on to. "I'd make time if you needed it. For anything."

"Even though I'm trouble?"

"I think we've established that I like the kind of trouble you bring to my life." The car shifted as he turned onto the street, and then twice more in quick succession as he navigated the few blocks to the county road that led to the city.

Once they were out of Wardham, he lifted her hand enough to slide his fingers through hers, and rubbed his thumb across her knuckles. She blinked her eyes open and took a deep breath.

"Maybe you should keep resting your eyes," he murmured. "You might not get a lot of sleep over the next few days."

"I'm okay."

"Do you want to call your parents again?"

She shook her head. "They're in the surgery waiting room. I'll email them once I know our flight details."

He squeezed her hand as his phone beeped. "Speak of the devil. Can you check that?"

She picked it up from the center console. She frowned at the display. "You have a text message from your ex-wife."

He chuckled, then abruptly stopped as he glanced over at her. "Hey, it's not—"

"No, it's okay. So very much none of my business." The words were flat and false on her tongue.

"Read it." Unmistakable challenge vibrated in two small words.

"Two seats reserved on Delta Flight 1403 at 3:40 pm out of DTW. I need the names from their passports." Oh. "You did this?"

"Susan's a travel agent." He shrugged. "It's not a big deal."

Hesitation held her back from stating unambiguously that it was a big deal. It was thoughtful and exactly what she needed. *He* was exactly what she needed. But that conversation would have to wait, for when she was strong enough to deal with the possibility that need might only run in one direction.

Because Paul wouldn't be moved by his wants. Hell, he probably would resist a need, too, unless she convinced him.

And that had never been her strong suit.

She'd never fought for anything. Never stood her ground, made her case, and damned the consequences. She'd hid behind what was safe and easy for her entire life, and look where it had led her.

Right to Paul.

Except it hadn't. She'd been frozen in time, and he'd stumbled across her at the same moment she'd started to thaw. And now her action plan, that she needed to follow, was going to take her away from him. *Just for a year.* God, she was going to give herself whiplash. Enough.

"That was nice of her."

"She's heard good things about you from Megan. She'd probably do it for you even if we weren't getting along."

"But you are?"

He reached out and entwined his fingers with hers again. "We are. Probably because of you."

"What did I do?"

"You set a good example." He cleared his throat. "That's probably a conversation best kept for another time."

Her lips curled into a slight smile. "No, I like where this is going. It's a good distraction for me, too. You're doing a public service by being nice to me."

He dropped their hands to rest on her knee, and the warmth of his forearm resting on top of hers made her stomach flip in the most pleasant way. "You taught me not to shy away from the tough conversations. To push through and expect something good on the other side."

———

SHE BIT HER LIP, and he silently cursed at himself. Now she was second guessing something in her head, and that wasn't where he wanted to go. He didn't want her doubting herself. He didn't want her thinking at all, but that was an impossible fight. Maybe a conversation about their relationship would be an acceptable distraction from what was looming in front of her in St. Louis. Even better if he could re-direct it to a lighthearted place. He'd hit the jackpot if he could give her a little confidence boost at the same time.

"Hey..." He flipped his hand over, releasing her fingers so he could squeeze her knee. "Where did I go wrong?"

"I don't always do that."

"The first time we met, you lurked in your front bushes, waiting to ambush me."

She jerked in her seat, and he chuckled. Mission accomplished. "That wasn't the first time we met."

"So you've said before. Why don't you enlighten me?"

Her knee bumped up into his palm as she twisted to look more fully at him, and he took the opportunity to twist his fingers up and under the bottom of her capris. Warm skin stretched over bone and muscle, providing an endless moving playground for his fingers to explore. Did she feel the same spark at the barest contact? Get wrapped up in the same compulsion to constantly touch, to find that physical connection no matter how futile any attempt at a relationship might be?

"There were a couple of times that I tried to talk to you before that afternoon."

He watched her out of the corner of his eye as she licked her lips, and if she wasn't in the middle of a family crisis, he'd have pulled over and done it for her. Kiss and lick and bite her lips until she was squirming in his lap, all hot and needy. He cleared his throat again. "I don't remember."

Her fingers danced against each other as she pulsed her hands in the air. "I wasn't successful. One time you were going out for a jog, and ran right past me."

"I don't believe it." At her confused look, he stroked his hand up and over her knee cap before squeezing her leg. Reassuring her, satisfying his own need to touch. Two birds, one stone. "Have you seen yourself? If I didn't notice you, it's because of all the fucked up shit in my head, darlin'. Nothing on you."

"What do—no. Never mind."

"It's okay, you can ask."

"It's none of my business."

What's mine is yours. The truth smacked him in the chest, and he had to fight to keep from visibly reacting. When had that happened? He'd been more open with Karen than anyone else in the past, but she still didn't know most of the messed up thoughts he had. And now he was an open book? Since when?

Since twelve hours earlier when he'd been balls deep in her, and decided he'd never give that up. Not for anything. Susan and Megan would have to deal. Hell, they'd probably both be pleased as punch. It would only be Karen that would take some convincing.

But he would. Because she was worth it.

Because he loved her.

Fuck.

Now was so not the time for dawning awareness. Right now, he needed to be a good friend. He needed to distract her until Windsor, then deliver her and her sister to the Detroit airport. When—fuck, *if*—her brother pulled through this and her family came out of this crisis without needing too much, then he could lay his feelings on the table. Make his case for a long-distance, take-it-slow-or-whatever, as-long-as-there-isn't-anyone-else relationship. He'd waited thirty-seven years for her, what was one more?

"Suffice it to say that I had a lot on my mind when I moved to Wardham, and I apologize sincerely for not noticing you sooner." He winked at her and squeezed her knee again before changing the subject reluctantly. "Do you know what name your sister would have on her passport? You should text Susan what she needs to know."

Another opportunity lost, his sub-conscious warned. *Shut up,* he argued back. *Stop thinking with your imaginary dick.*

15

ONE crying woman would put any man on edge. Two crying women, one of whom he loved, a new realization at that, and the other he'd never met before…it was enough to make Paul want to run for the hills, if only until the sobbing stopped. Except it was Karen, and what looked like Karen 2.0, from the small glimpse he got before the younger woman buried her face in her sister's shoulder. And they needed to get this shit out of their system before landing in St. Louis, so he stood there awkwardly with Audrey's friend Liza. She introduced herself while the sisters had their cathartic moment, which Paul appreciated. He quietly asked if Audrey's bags were handy, and Liza pointed to a backpack leaning against the wall. He loaded that into the trunk and checked his watch. Time to move them along.

After a quick check for passports and international calling plans, because someone had to be practical and it might as well be him, he loaded both women into the car and nodded his thanks at Liza.

Once across the border, it didn't take long to reach the airport. He didn't bother parking—their flight would be called soon enough, and he didn't know how Karen would want to play it in front of her sister. Instead, he stopped in the kiss and fly lane outside Departures, and turned to Karen just as she was reaching to touch his arm. Her pale cheeks and red-rimmed eyes reminded him she was on the edge, but her palm was warm and still against his skin.

"The flight details are in the email Susan sent," he started, deliberately sticking to the mundane. "You should double check you've got her number programmed into your phone."

She giggled, and he couldn't help but join her in finding that funny. Better than crying, he supposed. And maybe it would be good for them to be able to connect directly. Susan hadn't hesitated to help. She didn't even question why Paul was asking on Karen's behalf.

In the rear-view mirror, he caught Audrey watching him, eyes squinted in a deductive fashion. Instead of worry, relief crawled down the back of his neck and eased some of the tension that had taken up residence in his shoulders. While she was in St. Louis, Paul was going to have to talk to Megan about Karen. It was time for his daughter to know that he was dating again. Even if Karen didn't know it yet. He wasn't going to give up on them this time, no matter what barriers she threw in his path.

———

For Karen, the next three hours were a blur of waiting and rushing, impatience and frustrated self-censorship because no inconvenience or annoying airline procedure came close to what her brother was enduring. Getting to the hospital, blessedly without running into any paparazzi, and finally—finally—stumbling into the waiting room, it was like passing through a filter and everything else faded away. Their parents looked tired, and Audrey tugged on Karen's arm. As if she needed any encouragement to sprint across the room and wrap them in tight, never-let-go hugs.

"He's moved into the recovery unit." Karen brushed hair from her mother's face, a tender role-reversal moment that didn't go unnoticed by either of them before her mom continued, waving at the digital display high on one wall. "He's the third patient down on that list. The nurse warned us that the surgeons might not be able to immediately come and see us, but it should be soon."

"That gentleman over there—" Their father waved at a tall white haired man who returned the sentiment with a polite nod. "His wife is having her fourth operation in this hospital. He said no news is good news."

"Do you need anything? Want us to do a coffee run?" Audrey's voice was small but strong.

"No need, sweetie. That vending machine over there makes the most delicious cappuccinos."

Karen snorted, and from the look on Audrey's face she didn't quite believe it either. Their father chuckled under his breath— thank goodness for small miracles—and Karen made a silent vow to swallow whatever brown swill came out of that machine if it amused her parents.

From the doorway, the sound of someone clearing their throat made both young women jump, but their mother smoothly stepped between them and nodded at the two men in suits. "Welcome back, Oscar. We haven't heard from the surgeon yet, but he's been moved to recovery."

Oscar. One of them was her brother's agent. The other must be from the team.

"Thank you, Grace. You holding up?"

"Now that my daughters are here, absolutely."

"I just spoke with Davis, he's in Houston." Oscar flicked his wrist, revealing an extra-shiny watch. "Maybe taxiing out of Houston, his layover was only 40 minutes. He should be here in a couple hours."

Karen turned her face toward her mother and lowered her voice. "I saw a sign about visiting hours ending at 8:00 p.m., will that apply to Davis?"

Her mother nodded, her brows pinched together. "Not that he'll let that stop him, but I think so."

"Maybe we should get some hotel rooms?" *If there are any left.* Maybe they'd all have to cram into the RV.

"If it's not too forward, Ms. Miller, we've booked two suites at a hotel not far from here." The other man finally spoke. At Karen's raised eyebrow, he hastily added, "Sorry. I'm Mitchell. Mitchell Wagner. Director of Communications for the Coyotes."

She nodded and turned back to her mother and her father, who had joined them, forming a tight pack of Millers. Her dad passed her a surprisingly yummy smelling paper cup and she rolled her eyes at his smug expression before returning to the subject at hand. "That okay with you?"

"We're fine in the trailer," her mother murmured, but Audrey cut her off with a quick thanks to the men in suits.

"There's more to discuss in the coming days, of course—"

"And that can wait for those coming days." Oscar cut off the younger man, but before Karen could figure out where that had been heading, another young man, this one wearing scrubs and a matching hat and backwards gown, stepped into the waiting room and drifted his gaze toward her parents. Karen suddenly felt old, surrounded by professionals who looked a decade younger than her.

"Excuse me, are you the Miller family?" Her father stepped forward and nodded. "Follow me." He held up his hand as they stepped as one large group toward the door. "Family only, I'm sorry."

"My wife and daughters can all come?"

A quick nod and a swirl of blue fabric. Karen was glad to follow him across the main corridor and through a restricted access doorway. The *more to discuss* could happen after they'd processed whatever they were about to be told. On their timetable. On Chase's timetable. Not the team's, or his agent's, no matter how many hotel suites they booked.

He led them to a small, pleasantly appointed family meeting room. Once they were all inside, he gestured to the couch and chairs. "Please, have a seat. I'm Kevin, one of the OR nurses. The surgeons will be in to speak to you soon. I can tell you that the surgery went well, and as you know, Chad is in the recovery unit right now. Once you are done here, one of you can go and sit with him."

Karen reached out and squeezed her mom's hand. Grace Miller was vibrating with impatience. Thankfully, they didn't need to wait long. As promised, two more scrub-clad bodies soon whirled into the room and introduced themselves as two of the surgeons who had worked on Chase all afternoon.

The older doctor, tall and distinguished, introduced himself as the Chief of Orthopedic Surgery, and explained about the plates and screws that were holding together Chase's pelvis and one of his ankles, and how they repaired fractures in both legs. "He was lucky to avoid any damage to his internal organs. He doesn't need to spend any time in the ICU, but we will be monitoring him closely over the next forty-eight hours. After that, if all goes well, we'll start to discuss the next steps."

He stood, shook hands with Grace and Hank, then excused himself after reassuring them that he'd stay in close contact with the public affairs department and the hockey team, so the family wouldn't need to provide any medical details to the press.

After he left, the younger doctor explained she was a senior resident, the primary surgeon on Chase's ankle repair, and offered to answer any further questions they had about the surgeries and what was in his near future. Hank had the most questions, but Dr. Razvi answered them clearly and in language they all understood. It wasn't long before another knock on the door told them that Chase had moved from recovery to a private room in a step-down unit nearby.

After the surgeon left the room, they all let out a collective sigh. It could be so much worse, but would Chase feel the same way? As if she had the same thought, Karen's mother rose to leave, but Hank stood with her and pulled her into a fierce hug first. One of his hands squeezed the back of his wife's neck, the other stroked the small of her back, and, mouth to her ear, he whispered something private that visibly eased Grace's weariness. She nodded, and pulled away enough to stroke her husband's brow before setting her face into implacable mom mode.

Watching her parents comfort each other in small but familiar ways now carried more significance for Karen. If things were different, that could have been her and Paul in thirty years.

That was a depressing train of thought, and she was too darn tired to deal with it. If she entertained that resentment, she'd crawl inside herself and give up. They might not be able to have a forever love affair like her parents, but they had something, and she wasn't going to let go of that just because it wasn't everything she might want it to be.

Hearing his voice would help. Her gaze drifted to the large picture on the wall, a cell phone trapped behind a red crossed out circle, and puffed her cheeks out with a heavy sigh. Right. That wasn't going to happen.

"Come on, girls, let's head back to the waiting room, I'm sure they need this room for other families." Her dad held the door for them, and once they were across the hall again he turned all business. Hank Miller was back, and in charge. A weight lifted from Karen's shoulders, and she let herself be taken care of for a few minutes.

After dispensing Mitchell and Oscar on tasks, Hank opened his laptop and announced that Davis's flight would be landing on time, and they'd need a plan to sneak him into the hospital later. Audrey protested, and Karen smiled to herself. They'd both always been rule followers, Grace's good girls, both of them. But Davis and Chase were close, to each other and their father, who knew his hellions better than anyone. There was no point pretending their brother would wait until morning.

"He'll have no trouble getting past the nurses; or he will, but he'll get a few numbers and get a note to Chase either way." She rolled her eyes at her father's proud grin. "Seriously, Dad? Good lord. That's where they both get their false sense of invincibility. Jeez."

Hank ignored her verbal jab and lifted the computer instead. "Do either of you want to check your email?"

Audrey waved him off, but Karen gratefully accepted the offer. They'd never emailed before, but maybe Paul would have magically sourced her address the way he had her phone number earlier in their relationship.

Their relationship.

She stilled her fingers on the keyboard, hating the painful thump of hope in her chest at those two little words. Their weak-ass, limited-by-too-many-constraints, secret relationship. Nothing to get excited about.

But she did. Couldn't help it. For all of his protests, he was the best man she'd ever met, ever been with, and she'd dropped all of her defenses.

Now her expectations were sky-high. Crappity crap.

Even as she mentally scrambled to not care what she found, or didn't find, in her inbox, disappointment unfurled in her gut.

Stop it, she told herself, but it was no good. The page loaded, revealing a bunch of bookseller promotional messages and a single personalized note—from Carrie.

"Kar? Everything okay?"

She glanced up, blinking twice to focus on Audrey's furrowed brow and bright eyes. "Yeah." She closed the browser window. "Yep, everything is okay."

"Nothing from—"

"No." Karen shot her sister a sharp look. *Not in front of Dad.* Not at all, if she had her choice, but Audrey was a dog with a bone when she was curious. All she could do was postpone the inquisition.

Audrey shrugged her shoulders, like she didn't get why it was a big deal.

But Paul was a big deal. Maybe the only chance she'd ever have for a passionate affair. The thought of dating anyone else just made her sad. Sad that she hadn't finished her schooling a decade earlier, that she couldn't be the easy, always-present, flexible-life girlfriend that Paul needed right now. And deep down, sad that he couldn't be what she needed, either. It wasn't fair, when in every other way they seemed perfect for each other.

She felt like she was back in high school, riddled with hormones. Frustration bubbled hot and desperate inside her, her personal drama twisting around her fear and worry for her brother. When her mother reappeared in the waiting room door, this time with a tired but happy smile warming her face, some of Karen's anxiety faded, and she pushed the rest of her concerns away. First, she had a little brother to pick on for being a terrible driver. Then she could start to fix her own mess.

16

CHASE looked terrible, so she held off on teasing him. In the end, she didn't say much of anything, just squeezed his hand sixty thousand times and pretended to be brave. Audrey, who had cried all of her tears earlier, actually was brave, and managed to get their brother to crack a few smiles before sleep overtook him and they slipped out of his room.

The night nurse, a hockey fan with grown children of her own, pish-poshed when Grace tried to say goodnight, and promised to find a lie-flat recliner instead. The girls hovered in the hallway for a minute, in case their dad needed a ride, but he waved them on. "Davis will pick up a rental car—I'll wait here until he shows up and then head to hotel with him. It'll be a good excuse to get him up here."

At the hotel, Mitchell was waiting in the lobby. He straightened as they stepped through the revolving doors and offered a hesitant wave. He had a nerdy vulnerability now, out of Oscar's shadow, and Karen felt the sharp edge of her resistance to him soften. For a communications suit, he wasn't all that polished. And he looked genuinely relieved to see them.

"Mitchell, you didn't have to meet us here. I thought you'd

still be waiting at the hospital." Karen offered a small smile. "Not that there's anything that any of us can do right now, I suppose."

"Oscar's going to wait there overnight. I need to make some phone calls and that's easier from here. Did you have any difficulty getting away?"

Audrey shook her head. "No. The ward clerk went ahead of us and scouted a clear exit. She said there's only a couple of reporters in the lobby, and a hospital spokesperson is keeping them entertained."

He nodded. "I have a staff person liaising with the hospital. They're going to do a press conference tomorrow. With the series going to game seven, this is a minor story." He winced. "For the media, not for your family, of course."

Before Karen could assure him no offense had been taken, Audrey reached out, pressed a hand to his forearm and murmured the same thing. Mitchell swallowed hard and shifted ever so slightly. *Interesting.*

In the elevator, Karen snuck side glances at her not-so-little sister. Should she say something? Was it any of her business? Probably not, but maybe if it was a tit-for-tat exchange…

"So. Want to talk about guys?"

Audrey's gaze snapped up from her studious exploration of the geometrical pattern on the carpet. "Like that Paul guy?"

She laughed. "Sure. And maybe I'll play the big sister card and warn you about the dangers of flirting with nerdy older guys."

"I wasn't flirting! And he's not nerdy!" Audrey's eyes flashed wide and bright for a second, but narrowed as she mulled over the last bit. "He is older, though. And he probably wouldn't want to have a fling with Chase's little sister."

Ache pulsed in Karen's chest. When did her baby sister, who had been in grade one when Karen left home for university, grow up? But that wasn't her sole cause for concern. What had she been thinking, trying to play it fast and loose with Paul? He'd held her off for good reason. And after one night and an emotionally needy morning, she'd immediately leapt to a plan that disrespected his carefully constructed boundaries.

A fling was a terrible idea.

"Maybe for you."

Karen jerked her spine straight. "Did I say that out loud?"

The elevator doors opened and Audrey held her hand over the gap, waving her off first. "Mitchell looks at me like he'd be happy to see me naked and make it worth my time. He's fling material. Paul looks at you…"

Karen's pulse picked up. "How does he look at me?"

"Like you're the most precious thing in the world, and he doesn't quite know what to do about that." Audrey wrinkled her nose. "I mean that last bit in a good way. Like he can't believe he's the guy who gets to be with you."

If only. "Up until yesterday, he wasn't. And even today, I'm not sure where we stand."

"What happened?"

"It's a long story." Their suite was at the end of the hall. Karen slid her card into the reader and pushed the door open.

They fumbled for lights, unpacked, used the bathroom and flopped on the matching double beds before Audrey cleared her throat.

"What?"

"I'm waiting for the long story. The tale of woe that will warn me off an ill-advised fling with Nerdy Mitchell."

"How is that guy the Director of Communications for an NHL team?" Karen laughed gently. "I guess he has a certain disarming charm."

"I'm pretty sure he's more nerdy around me than other people."

"Wow, that's…confident."

"Today wasn't the first time we've met. I've seen him a few times at games. He looks at me, a lot." Audrey grinned. "Now that we know Chase is going to be okay, I feel like this could be an opportunity."

"No." Karen shook her head from side to side, but both her words and her action lacked conviction. Who was she to give advice, on flings, or relationships…or anything, really? "I don't know. It seems like a bad idea."

"It's a terrible idea. I'm thinking about it anyway."

"Seriously, when did you turn into a woman?"

"A while ago."

"Hmmm."

"When did you fall in love with Paul?"

"A while ago." With a groan, Karen pressed the heels of her hands into her eye sockets. Maybe if she pressed hard enough, she'd pass out, and wake up back in Wardham. Maybe this whole sad, mixed-up day was a nightmare.

"So what's the problem?"

"He has a ten-year-old daughter, and between work and trying to be an active part in her life, he can't have a long-distance relationship for the next year."

"And you're definitely leaving."

"Yeah." Oh, the irony. "And that's because of him, you know? He pushed me to admit I wanted more out of life. One of the first times we ever talked, I spilled my guts about coming home that Christmas and never going back. Told him about the store, and Mom and Dad, and finally admitted I wanted the grand adventure I'd missed out on in my twenties."

"It's more than just school and a career change?"

No, it wouldn't be. She just wasn't cut out for that lifestyle. She couldn't be anything but the good girl, no matter how much she tried. Being trouble for Paul was as far as her bad girl career would ever extend. "That was the idea."

Audrey didn't say anything for a while, and Karen rolled over to check if her sister had fallen asleep. Instead, she was frowning up at the ceiling. "Do you think I'm a slut?"

"Because of Mitchell? God, no."

"But you never did anything like that…"

"Because I'm a different person than you. My choices aren't

better or worse, they're just…well, they're not even really choices. It's just how I am. And…" Audrey had confided in her. This secret would be safe, but it still pushed her outside her comfort zone to share it. "I've been a little slutty myself, lately."

"I thought you said a fling was a bad idea?"

"It is. You might accidentally fall in love." That ache returned, spreading now from her chest to unsettle her stomach. How was she going to deal with that? As if on cue, her phone rang. Still too early for Davis to have landed. With a twisted combination of anticipation and fear, she glanced at the display screen. Paul's name glowed, his number searing itself into her vision.

"That him?"

"Yeah."

"Why aren't you answering?"

"I don't know."

HE THOUGHT about calling again before his shift started, but it was early.

He hadn't slept well, rousing frequently to check his phone and wonder why she hadn't called. He knew that caring was a dangerous path to go down, but he'd made that choice a long time ago. It had just been pushed into overdrive yesterday, when his protective instincts kicked in. And throughout the night, not once had he thought it was a mistake to worry about Karen. To want to make her problems better, and be there for her to vent when he couldn't actually be the remedy himself. Even when he'd realized she wasn't going to call him back, that she didn't need him to be all of that for her, it didn't register as a problem.

But now in the light of day, he knew he'd find a way to sabotage himself. Any minute now, that autopilot would shut off and the fear that had permanent residence in his neocortex would take over.

He'd done some things he wasn't proud of after his divorce.

Regrettable one night stands, blown commitments with Susan and work, a few painful nights of trying to reclaim a youth he'd never had in the first place, and worst of all, he missed the better part of four years of Megan's life while he was stuck at the point of being left and knowing it had been his fault. It took him too damn long to shake off the fog of self-recrimination. He'd been around, but barely, and he didn't blame Susan for calling him on that bullshit.

But her doubt that he could turn it around, even as he did, took hold in his brain, and now the only lingering effect of his divorce and the aftermath was a hobbling sense that he would never be good enough. That he would inevitably fuck up any good that came into his life.

And Karen was good. Pure goodness, and he didn't deserve her.

She definitely deserved better than him, so it was too bad that he'd gone and fallen in love with her.

Jesus. That had been easier to admit yesterday, with the adrenaline rush of needing to take care of her. Now his stomach pitched wildly while a small, ugly voice inside warned he would break her heart and incur the wrath of a small but mighty town.

But there was no way he was letting her go. He had no idea how he'd voiced a suggestion that she hold off for a better man. Fuck that shit. The thought of Karen winding her long, gorgeous limbs around someone else had him seeing red.

There was only one thing to be done about that. He picked up his phone and dialed the familiar number. "I'm sorry for calling so early. I need to ask another favour."

"Who are you, and what have you done with Paul Reynolds?" Susan's voice was still sleepy, and the sarcasm was gentle, but it was still there.

"Sus—"

"I'm sorry. Of course, what do you need at…quarter after six in the morning?"

He should have waited until a more reasonable hour. "I need to talk to Megan. Not now, I mean—I'm going to work in a few minutes. But can she stay up a bit late tonight? I could probably be in the city by eight. I can talk to her at your house, if you'd rather."

"Is this about Karen?"

Tension coiled tight around his spine and up his neck. "Yes, is that a problem?"

"God, no." His ex sighed, and an awkward silence stretched between them. "I'm not sure what to say to reassure you that I'm not going to use a relationship against you. Have I not been supportive so far?"

She had. She'd actually been way more understanding than she needed to be. "I really appreciate you organizing those tickets for her yesterday."

"Then what's the problem?"

"Maybe there's too much history between us."

"But it's just that, history. The last couple of years have been good."

"Then why did it take so long to settle the custody challenge?" The question came out before he could censor himself. He winced and closed his eyes, but she surprised him.

"I owe you an apology for that. I was angry and at the end of my rope, but you pulled your act together a lot faster than I gave you credit for. Faster than maybe you've given yourself credit, too." Susan gentled her voice again. "Anyone else in your shoes would have lashed out at me. I know I pissed you off, but you handled it well. Maybe too well. You gotta stop beating yourself up for what happened after the divorce."

"I was a dick to you, and a terrible father to Megan." And he still hadn't forgiven himself.

"*Was* being the operative word. You're as good an ex-husband as a woman could ask for, and I don't need to tell you you're a good father. Right? I don't need to?"

"Right. But..." Admitting this to Susan instead of Karen felt like a bit of a betrayal, but it was probably the last confidence he'd ever share with his ex-wife, and she had a unique insight. "Can I juggle being a good father and a good boyfriend at the same time?"

Susan laughed, starting with a snort, then a single hoot, and when he protested, she dissolved into hysterics. It took her a solid minute to compose herself, and then it was only to tell him he was an idiot before laughing again. "You're a thirty-seven-year-old man, Paul. You were a police detective for five years, and you've spent, what, fifteen years total critically observing human behaviour? How many people do you know who aren't capable of managing adult relationships?"

When she said it like that… "Okay, I'm an idiot."

"That's okay, you're someone else's idiot now."

"Gee, thanks."

"No problem." She glibly shifted subjects back to the original question. "You can come over tonight. You can stay, or take Meg out, whatever you'd rather."

After hanging up, he headed to work, knowing that he'd need to do something routine all day. His mind was going to be occupied with how to handle two very important conversations.

17

K AREN woke up early, before Audrey, and was about to put on a pot of coffee in the kitchenette when a knock sounded at the door.

She would have been happy to see her baby brother anyway, but as he carried a tray of steaming lattes, she actually cheered. Her father followed Davis into their room, declaring it was time for a family meeting.

Chase would be staying in St. Louis for at least a week, probably a couple, until the rehab team was confident he could continue recuperating at home. By home, Chase meant Wardham. He wouldn't need to return to Phoenix until the end of the summer anyway, even if he would be playing next year, which was pretty unlikely, but an undercurrent of something else was laced through the instruction. Davis knew more than he was letting on, but once again, it seemed like a conversation maybe not to have in front of their father.

When Audrey paused the meeting so she could drink her coffee and wake up, and Hank called the hospital to check in with Grace, Karen finally sent Paul a brief text message. Sorry, swamped here, but everything is okay. Or will be. Should be home in a few days.

By the time they had a plan ironed out—Karen and Audrey would drive the RV back, and their parents would stick around for a bit longer, then travel either with Chase or just in advance of him—Paul had sent a short and sweet response, telling her to call any time. Reading between the lines, she guessed he was busy, and took the weenie way out by calling him right then, knowing he wouldn't be able to talk long.

Hearing his voice was a punch in the gut. How was she going to leave him? It had only been a day, and she already ached to feel his warm skin beneath her fingers. Rest her head on his shoulder and breathe in his scent. He'd know without prompting that she'd want to talk, or not, and how was she going to live without all of that for a year?

Forever, really. Because what were the chances that his life would pause while she was away?

Too quickly, he had to end the call, and she was left holding her phone, alone in a hotel room in St. Louis, wishing so much could be different.

———

THE NEXT TWO days flew by, and before she knew it, Karen was riding shotgun as her twenty-one-year-old sister steered their parents' RV northwest on the I-70. She'd offer to give Audrey a break in Indianapolis, but she doubted her sister would relinquish control—of the vehicle, or the tunes. Karen would usually listen to country, but she had to admit, Audrey's old school hip hop mix provided the perfect road trip soundtrack.

As they bounced along to Salt n Pepa, Karen shook off her worry about her parents and brother, because they were going to be fine—probably grumpy as all get out by the end of this, but given the extent of his injuries, that Chase was going to walk again was a miracle. Now she had to return to real life.

Her heart skipped a bit at the thought of returning to Paul, as well, but that thrill was neatly coupled to worry and doubt now, after a few days of missed calls, short conversations and brief texts. Her guilt at avoiding the necessary conversation was probably feeding into her fear, but she was starting to think that Paul was doing the exact same thing.

But Paul wasn't the sum total of her life in Wardham. Or beyond—she needed to make a decision about which school, and soon. And her first task as soon as they were back home would be interviewing some of the interested tenants for her house, then figuring out what she'd move with her and what she'd need to put into storage.

She pulled out her tablet and made a to-do list. Satisfied for the interim, she flipped over to her e-book reader app and sank into the latest Wings of Woden tome. Before she knew it, she'd reached the end of the dragon's journey home, and when she looked up, they were at the halfway point in their own journey.

After four hours of driving, Audrey was content to switch spots, even if it meant the soundtrack shifted to Luke Bryan and Little Big Town. By the time they crossed the border, with ease thanks to Hanks' careful organization of the RV's documentation, they were both sick of driving and music of all stripes. The last few minutes of their drive were spent in solemn quiet. Audrey seemed reluctant to head to her dorm, so Karen suggested she come home to Wardham for the night and she could drive her back the next morning for class.

"You don't want to see Paul tonight?"

"If he's home, I probably will. If he's not..." If he wasn't, her sister's unexpectedly understanding company would be appreciated. Karen sighed.

"If he's not, we'll eat ice cream and watch Sixteen Candles."

"I don't think I own that."

Audrey snorted and rolled her eyes. "Hello? Age of the internet? Don't you have Netflix?"

"No, but I'm guessing I will by the end of the night."

"Damn straight."

Normally there was no overnight parking in Wardham, but

Karen figured no one would ticket Chase Miller's parents' RV, which there was no doubt this was, with the Proud Coyote Parents bumper stickers and custom stick figure decals. Davis and Audrey's caricatures were playing volleyball, Karen was reading a book, and Chase wore his jersey. Somehow it wasn't nearly as awful as it sounded. It was mostly wonderful, and any residual embarrassment faded when she thought of how earnestly her family supported each other the last few days. Always, actually. And she'd resisted that all-consuming love.

Because she didn't deserve it.

"Kar? We gonna go inside?"

She blinked and drew in a shaky breath. They were sitting at the curb in front of her house. She nodded, and after giving her a strange look, Audrey climbed out of the RV, groaning as she stretched her legs. Karen followed, feeling similarly achy, but glad to be home.

Paul's house was dark, but her front porch light was on. Had she done that when she left?

Inside, they found a note from Carrie letting them know the milk in the fridge was fresh—so Karen made hot chocolate to go with the basket of muffins her best friend had left as well.

She didn't resist Carrie's love. Or Evie's.

What made her family different?

What made Paul different?

"You've drifted again, Kar." Audrey took the tray Karen had set on the counter, loaded up the steaming mugs and plate of muffins, and led the way into the living room. "I've hooked my laptop up to your computer, so we'll use my Netflix account for now, but after tonight you'll want to set up your own, I'm sure."

Karen settled on the couch, nodding whenever Audrey looked over for confirmation that she was following the instructions. She totally wasn't, of course. "Hey," she interrupted. "We should text Davis and let him know we got home safely."

"Already done, and he responded, even though he isn't

supposed to have his phone on at the hospital. He's kicking Chase's ass at cards, apparently."

"Not fair, picking on the invalid."

"Like you wouldn't do the same thing."

"True story. I guess we'll have our turn when he comes home. Speaking of which…he's going to have to stay in the main house, no way he can get up the stairs to the loft." Their parents lived on a few acres just outside of town, on the lake. A few years earlier, when Chase got serious enough with a girlfriend to bring her home for a week, he had a contractor renovate what they affectionately called The Barn, but was really a glorified utility shed with an upper level. Now that loft was insulated for year-round comfort, had a nicer master bathroom than the main house, and was Chase's home while in Wardham. Close enough that he could eat his mother's food, but still have privacy.

"Yeesh. Even our momma's boy is going to find that chafes a bit." Audrey laughed at Karen's shocked expression. "What? He totally is."

"I thought I was the only one who saw that." She took a sip of hot chocolate. "It's probably because he left home so young."

"I don't remember." Audrey had just been a preschooler when Chase was first drafted into junior league hockey and moved across the province.

"It wasn't a big deal, Mom and Dad were so supportive. Davis got his own room, I didn't have to share the car on weekends. I don't mean it like it's a bad thing…just a thing."

"I always thought it was strange that he didn't mind them following him around in their RV."

Karen snorted, then sputtered as hot chocolate went up her nose. "Aren't you snarky tonight, eh?"

"Maybe it's a coping strategy."

"No, I think it's who you are." She grinned at her little sister. "I like it."

"Ha. Good. Movie time?"

Karen nodded, but a knock at the back door caused her to pause that thought. "Hang on."

"If it's Paul, I'm starting without you," Audrey shouted as Karen moved down the hall.

It was.

Her heart leapt into her throat.

She stepped out onto the deck and tugged the door shut behind her. Dusk had faded to dark, but the night was alive with chirping crickets and fragrant flowers. Despite the warm summer air, she shivered as the man she'd had on her mind for far too long stepped closer.

"Hey. You're back." His gaze swept over her face, warm and interested, and a sweet tingle started at the base of her neck.

"I am." She smiled. "And you're home."

"I am. With Megan." He nodded to a light on the second floor of his house. "Do you want to come over and hang out with us?"

"I would—I do—but my sister's here tonight. We're going to watch a movie. Do you guys want to join us?" Audrey wouldn't mind. She'd probably ask leading and slightly inappropriate questions, but she'd toe the line in front of Megan.

"What movie?"

She laughed. "Sixteen Candles."

He grinned, then reached up and laced his fingers into her hair, gently cupping the back of her neck at the same time. "Maybe we should do our own things tonight…but can you spare a few minutes now?"

Her breasts grew heavy at the thought of what Paul could do in a few minutes under the cover of darkness. As if he sensed her nipples tightening on demand, he closed the final gap between them, brushing her waist with his other palm, then the side swell of her breast. Could he feel her heart pounding?

"I've missed you, Karen." He brushed his lips across hers. "I'm sorry we haven't had more of a chance to talk."

"It's okay," she whispered. "It's just nice to see you now."

"Nice isn't how I would describe it," he growled, kissing her again, this time with less restraint and more honest hunger. "God, your mouth."

"Yeah?"

"Oh, yeah." The third kiss lingered on her lips, leaving behind a promise that she had no doubt he'd follow through on. Whatever happened at the end of the summer, there was going to be more of that before they were done.

"Listen—" From her back pocket, her phone rang, cutting him off. She gave him an apologetic squeeze before answering it.

———

FROM KAREN'S ONE-SIDED CONVERSATION, it sounded like she had a potential tenant coming to see the house the next day. As she chatted about references and deposits, he eased his way around her body until her back was pressed against his front, and he wrapped his arms around her waist, burying his face in her hair.

He'd gotten used to having her next door. It would be strange not being able to look out the window and know if she was around. It would make it that much more complicated to spend time together when she came home from school. He wouldn't be able to steal five minutes like this while Megan got ready for bed. She'd stay at her parents' place on the outskirts of town, and he'd have no idea if she was up late, or early. Would anyone notice when she got stressed out?

Maybe she could stay with him.

God, he was going about this all the wrong ways. That would just scare her off, make her think he ran hot and cold and didn't know what he really wanted.

He might be scared shitless at the thought of messing this up, but there was no doubt in his mind what he wanted. Karen, in his life, as much as her life allowed.

She ended the call and tipped her head sideways so he could see her profile. "Do you know the Wagners?"

He shook his head, enjoying the rub of her skin under his

nose. She hadn't used her regular shampoo, this was something generic, the hotel shampoo probably. A pleasant, mildly citrus, clean smell, but not Karen. But her skin smelled just right, and if he nibbled…yeah, it tasted perfect, too.

"Paul! Focus." She twisted in his arms and grinned. "One of the Wagner kids works for me at the grocery store. He's the youngest of five, and one of his older brothers is looking to rent a house with his girlfriend. I'll still need to meet them to make it official, but I think I've found a tenant!"

"That's great." He tipped her head back and feathered kisses down her neck, bending his knees as he reached her collarbone. "Want to meet back here after our housemates fall asleep, and we can celebrate properly?"

"Mmmm." She half-groaned, half-sighed under his mouth, and he was tempted to push her into the shadows, but she stepped back. His dick ached hot and heavy, more so again when she dropped her eyes to take in his obvious want of her. A wicked smile, pure pleasure, curled up her face, and he leaned in for one final taste.

"Two hours?" She nodded. "Okay, see you then. Wear a skirt."

18

———

"HOW'S Karen's brother?" Megan sat cross-legged on her bed.

"I didn't ask. Her sister is visiting for the night, and they were about to watch a movie, so I just said hi." Paul relaxed against the doorframe. "And she said to say hi to you, as well. Maybe we can do something, the three of us, tomorrow or the next day."

"Did you ask her out yet?"

He chuckled. "No, not yet."

"You can't take her for granted, Dad. What if someone else asks her out first?"

Then he'd find himself on the wrong side of the law, most likely. "I don't think that's a concern, sweetheart."

"Uh, really? Have you seen Karen? She's hot. And nice. And she likes books. I'm pretty sure a lot of guys ask her out."

He would've thought so, too, but it didn't seem to be the case. That was a puzzle that he'd like to figure out. Maybe after he'd secured the title of exclusive boyfriend, though. He wasn't a martyr.

"I'm going to ask her out on a real date, real soon. For now, we're just going to play it cool and hang out with her as friends, okay?"

"Please, I saw you kiss her."

Shit. What had he been thinking? Of course Megan would be nosy. No, not nosy. Normally curious. Shit, fuck, damn...

"Stop swearing in your head." His ten-year-old was too clever by half.

"Don't use my mind reading tricks against me."

"It's not mind-reading, just basic psychology." Meg parroted back his oft-quoted line at him, and they both laughed, but Paul quickly sobered up and moved to join his daughter on her bed.

"Hey, seriously. I'm sorry that you saw me kiss Karen."

"Why?"

An excellent question.

"Because I want to do this right. Like I told you the other night, I'm serious about wanting to see her more, be her boyfriend, go on dates. Because she deserves that kind of respect. And you do, too."

"It's just a bit of kissing, Dad. I mean, I think it's pretty gross, but I know that when I'm grown up a bit more, I'll want to kiss people."

"Oh god, you're going to give me a heart attack." He laid his hands over his chest in mock horror. "You talk to your mom about stuff like this?"

"Yep. She's the one who told me that kissing is okay. I mean, more okay than other stuff."

"What do you mean?" Paul willed himself the courage to be brave and answer appropriately, no matter where this conversation went.

"You know, other stuff. Mom said that if anyone talks to me about sex, that I should tell her, or you, or someone safe like Karen. But if a boy wanted to kiss me, and I wanted him to kiss me, then that was okay, because it's normal and healthy."

"Your mom is pretty smart."

"I know. She takes after me." Megan snorted as she crawled under her covers, pushing him off her bed in the process. "I'm going to read for a bit, okay?"

"Sure. Nighty night."

"Daaa-ad!"

"Whatever, kiddo. You're still my little girl." He patted her foot and headed for the door.

———

AUDREY FELL asleep before Jake got to the church, but roused in time to mouth the final few lines of dialogue with Karen. Then she stumbled to the spare room and fell asleep again, still in her clothes. There were worse things.

Karen rinsed their mugs and left them in the sink to wash properly the next day. She was itching to see Paul. She was about to head upstairs to put on a sundress when he knocked at the door for the second time that night.

"Hey, that was sooner than I expected."

"I came over as soon as Meg fell asleep."

She laced her arms around his shoulders. "Book on her face?"

"You know it. I just turned out her light."

"She's such a good kid."

He nodded. "But growing up way too fast. She saw us kissing tonight, and that led to a sex talk, and oh my god, I'm so not ready for that."

"Crap. It's always out of the blue, isn't it?" She tipped her forehead into his neck and laughed softly. "I guess that puts a damper on your libido for the night, huh?"

He groaned and pulled her tight against his body. "Just about the only thing that could, darlin'."

"It's okay, I'm tired."

"I wish you could come over and sleep in my bed."

"You are a very nice body pillow, I must admit."

"Want a neck rub? Come sit on the deck with me for a few minutes before you turn in."

She couldn't think of anything better.

———

THE NEXT MORNING, Audrey drove the RV to their parent's place, and Karen followed her. After parking it on the concrete pad behind the loft, they headed for the city.

Davis called with an update that wasn't much of an update, but at least the holding pattern was better than full-out crisis. It was hard to leave Audrey after that call, it seemed like they should stick together longer, but Audrey had class and Karen had potential tenants to meet. A quick glance at the clock told her she had time to hit the Victoria's Secret outlet shop, though, and so she did. Given that Megan was staying with Paul for almost a week, due to summer holidays, she wasn't sure when she'd get a chance to share her new finds, but the thought of his fingers slipping inside her waistband and brushing over new lace gave her a thrill all by itself.

And this was what life would be, dating a single dad. And it didn't matter if something else would be different, more time or less, because this was all she wanted. Paul, however she could get him.

She thought about grabbing a Starbucks for the drive, but she owed Carrie a visit, and two back-to-back lattes would have her up all night. Not getting one at Bun was out of the question, of course. She shifted into sixth gear, thankful that Paul wasn't working today. It would be awkward to get a speeding ticket from a potential boyfriend.

The shop smelled like lemon glaze, and Carrie reached for the milk pitcher as soon as she stepped in the door. She knew the drill. "Welcome home, Hulkster!"

"Thank you muchly. And thanks for the muffins, Audrey stayed over last night and we devoured them all."

"It was the least I could do. Can I ask how Chase is? I saw a bit of a press conference this morning, but they didn't say much."

Karen shrugged. "Yep, that's about the sum of it. I think we'll know more at the end of the week, he'll have another round of x-rays then."

"Tell your mom I'm thinking of her."

Carrie had two little kids, and her five year old son was itching to play hockey, just like Chase Miller. Carrie could probably very well imagine what Karen's mom was going through.

Karen sank onto one of the barstools and gratefully accepted the latte her friend slid across the counter. Would she have greater insight into her mother's situation if she had kids herself? Having kids had always seemed a useless academic question in the past— one would need a serious boyfriend first—but now she was looking, for the first time, at that possibility, but with someone who'd already been there, done that. Falling in love with Paul might be sealing her future of never having kids.

That was an unexpectedly heavy place for her thoughts to turn. Karen sighed and rubbed her brow.

"Penny for your thoughts."

"Too many thoughts, not enough pennies. Not the right place for it, either," Karen whispered the last bit as a customer came in.

Carrie boxed up their requested dozen muffins, made change quickly and with an inordinate amount of cheer, then was back before Karen had any further chance to self-analyze.

"I think we need another girls' night to properly debrief. I have to go meet one of the Wagner kids, he might rent my house while I'm gone. Then I have to do the bookmobile rounds."

"Oh honey, of course. Laney's in town for a couple more days, could we invite her, too?" Carrie waved her hands in the air. "Never mind, I'm sure Evie won't mind keeping it small."

"No, it's okay. Actually, since I missed their engagement party, it would be good to catch up. And I have some questions for her about Chase's recovery." Karen picked up her coffee and pushed away from the counter. "Mmmm. And you know, maybe we should invite Mari. She's always good for a chat, and might make Laney feel a little less like a fourth wheel."

"If Mari comes, she'll probably want to invite Stella. The poor girl never gets away from the farm."

A big, joyous estrogen fest sounded like just the ticket. "The more the merrier."

As she headed home, she noticed a missed text message from Paul, inviting her over for dinner, then a second message rolled in, identifying the texter as Megan using her dad's phone. When the phone rang a minute later, she answered with a laugh. "She stole your technology, eh?"

"Yep." Desire and confusion warred inside her at the sound of his voice, rich and calm. Could it really be this simple? Surely not. And her fleeting thought about the future, and what may or may not be, would that snowball into a problem before they ever got off the ground as a couple? And yet his voice... "So, we've invited you over for dinner. Do you like chicken?"

"I like everything. Except capers."

"Don't worry, we're a caper-free house."

"Okay."

"Okay. Six?"

"Can it be a bit later? I've got books to deliver to people."

"Seven."

"Meg won't mind?" She was almost home. It was silly, having this conversation on the phone, really.

"Not a bit."

He waved through his front window as she hung up, but her potential tenants were waiting on her porch, so she just nodded and turned her attention to Mitchell's older brother Gavin and his girlfriend Stacey, who were pleased as punch at her asking price for rent, but had some trouble with moving at the start of September. Stacey was currently in a studio apartment, with furniture, and needed to be out by the end of July, just three weeks away. They could stay with Gavin's parents for a bit, but...

"Say no more, I get it. At the very least, you can put your furniture in my garage, or the spare room. That's what I was going to do, to make room for your stuff. We'll sort it out."

"Thank you, Karen." The look shared between the young, eager lovers at the prospect of being mere weeks away from living together sent a pang of longing through her gut. At the bare minimum, if everything went well, she was a year away from being free and clear to hope for the same thing.

Baby steps. First, dinner with his daughter, who saw them kissing last night, and still wanted to spend them with her. Panic about a potential future could wait until some point after that.

After Gavin and Stacey took off, probably to go screw like bunnies from the way they were groping each other on the way out, Karen turned her attention to the bags of large print and audio books, as well as regular paperbacks, that she'd take around to the two retirement homes and a number of Wardham residents who still lived on their own but had trouble getting to the library on a regular basis.

For a while, she and Mildred had tried using the library resources for this project, but the logistics got a bit difficult as the list of readers grew. Waiving late fees, keeping track of library cards...a few sheets of paperwork turned into a heavy binder, and that wasn't in the spirit of fun reading. Karen called it a bookmobile, but it was really just a few bags of books in her trunk. A lean, mean, lending machine. And after word got out that she was looking for books to share with community members with accessibility issues, donations piled in, and continued to show up on her doorstep from time to time. Most of the time, she didn't even bother signing books out for people, just left something they might like and took back what she recognized as having been borrowed before. Each one had a large sticker on the back with her address and phone number, and every few months she added another tote bag to her collection, so from an inventory management perspective, she was quite content with the laissez-faire approach.

So why couldn't she let go and just let whatever would be with Paul...just be? See what would happen over time, organically? Something was happening, that was for sure. Something that would have to end, or be put on hold, by the end of the summer. And the queasy feeling in the pit of her stomach told her it might not be exactly what she wanted.

Too bad she couldn't change that without sacrificing her second chance at her dream career.

19

———

DINNER had been nice. Really nice, but it would have been better if Karen hadn't headed to bed—at her house, alone—at the same time Megan did.

Paul didn't know what to make of that. He'd been so worried about sending mixed messages himself that he was just catching on to the fact that Karen might not be on totally sure footing with regard to their relationship, either. The night before, they'd been a few seconds away from ripping each other's clothes off. That passion, even if tempered by real life, meant something. The lift in her voice when he called her. That meant something, too. Throughout dinner, he'd look up and catch her watching him, her gaze hot and full of feeling.

Yeah, there were an abundance of feelings between them. But they weren't talking about them.

They still hadn't been on a formal date. He needed to get on that. He did his best thinking while pounding out a few miles on a run. He didn't have a treadmill, and didn't want to leave Megan alone in the house, so a hard workout would have to be an acceptable substitute.

He tossed his portable pull-up bar into the doorway between the living room and the hallway, and stripped off his shirt.

One. Two. Three.

With each lift, he considered and rejected date options. This wasn't about determining compatibility. There was no measure of their chemistry required. This was a date they'd tell their grandchildren about. It needed to be special.

Four. Five. Six.

Not dinner, or a movie. Maybe a baseball game? Close, but something was missing. He could picture them at a game, pressing their heads together, making silly faces for a double self-portrait. One arm wrapped around Karen, pulling her in tight to his side, the other outstretched, holding the camera at an angle to secretly make sure to include her cleavage in the shot.

He laughed to himself and lost count, which seemed like a good point to switch to crunches. He dropped to the floor and started in on his abdominal muscles. Crunches first, then oblique side lifts. He grabbed a dumbbell from under the couch to ramp up the intensity, pinning it between his ankles for the second round.

Good, hard sweat started to roll down his back as he went back to the pull up bar for another set of reps, and as his muscles burned, clarity dawned. He pulled his boxing bag from the hall closet and took down the pull up bar, hanging the bag from the eye-hook in the middle of the doorway. It wasn't pretty, but it kept him in shape, and from time to time, got him very much on the right track with a hard-to-fix problem.

Not that Karen was a problem. Jab. Jab. Punch.

Except for the part where she didn't want to hang around after Megan went to bed. That was—

"Do you always workout half-naked?"

He spun around, fists at his side. He'd been so inside his head he hadn't heard the back door open. "You came back."

She moved closer, pausing to pick up his water bottle. She passed it over, and he took a big sip. "I did. I thought I was tired, but I couldn't settle."

She'd changed into cotton shorts and a structured tank top, and it dawned on him that she might just be naked underneath both.

"Give me a second to have a shower, then we could watch a movie or something."

"Megan's asleep upstairs?"

"Yeah. The *or something* would have to be under a blanket and really quiet." He winced. "Was that really sleazy? I'm a bit desperate to get you naked again, the line of propriety is blurry for me right now."

She sucked in a breath and held it for a second before letting the dam burst. "You, too? Oh, good. I thought I was a bit pathetic for coming over here for what amounts to a booty call while your daughter sleeps upstairs. Because really, that's a terrible idea, right?"

"It's not a terrible idea for me to fool around on the couch with my girlfriend. First base has already been okayed by Megan." And as he said *that*, his hard-on disappeared and he grimaced. Great. Cock blocking himself again.

She reached out and entwined their fingers together, ignoring his repeated comment about needing a shower. "I like your sweat, remember? You are so unbelievably hot right now, it makes me—" She cut herself off. "Sorry, I won't go down that road if you're not comfortable with us doing anything down here while she's upstairs."

At some point, he wanted Karen in his bed every night. If he was totally honest, that point was right now. A tremor wracked through his body.

Fuck it. Fear could taking a flying leap. He had a claim to stake. "She knows I love you. This isn't a booty call, and we don't have anything to be ashamed of." He moved to pull her hard against his body, but her hands came up between them and pressed a warning into his chest.

He'd missed something. Her face had blanched, her eyes were

wide, and it took him a moment. He re-wound his words as he took a deep breath, and heard himself tell Karen that he loved her in the most off-hand way just as she pushed herself away from him. His hands, slick with sweat, grasped at her waist, but she had moved too quickly.

She paced a few steps away, then turned around, still speechless. Her thoughts were spinning a mile a minute, though, and he watched her face and body language as she processed. His first instinct was to spit out a bunch of other stuff, provide some context for the words that he'd felt long enough to get sloppy and share at the wrong moment. But there, it was out in the open.

And she didn't hate it, which was good. But she was torn, that much was obvious. Why?

"I'm leaving at the end of the summer." Her lips barely moved, and the words slipped out. He wasn't the only one who'd been wrapped up in fear, apparently. Damn.

"Baby. That's okay." He crossed the room in two long steps and wrapped her in a tight hug. "I haven't forgotten about school. That's going to be hard as hell, but we'll figure something out."

"Just like that?" She shook her head. "I can't disrupt your life like that. Or Megan's."

He hadn't thought this through. He'd do a much better job convincing her upstairs. In his bed. "Come on."

She protested as he tugged her into the hall. "No! Paul…"

"Shhh. I'm sneaking you into my room."

Megan's room was at the front of the house, and his was at the back. Between them was a small room he'd filled with all the boxes Karen had made him move out of his garage, but that was originally going to be an office, and beside that was the bathroom. He pointed Karen to his bed, and pantomimed that she should take off her clothes. She rolled her eyes and stayed dressed as he crept down the hall to make sure Megan was asleep. He switched on the fan on her dresser, grateful for the white noise, and clicked her door closed.

Back in his room, he did the same thing, and rolled up a towel to cover the gap between his door and the floor.

"Why do I think this isn't the first time you've snuck a girl into your room?" Karen hissed gently, her eyes narrowed. Her lips betrayed her interest, though, and she lifted her arms agreeably when he gripped the bottom of her tank top and lifted.

"Not in twenty years."

"Really? I thought..." Karen licked her lips. "Never mind, don't want to know right now."

He stilled for a moment, quickly rifling through the options. Shit. "You thought my reluctance to date again was because Megan had been exposed to my dating in the past."

"Well, yeah."

"Not exactly. Not like this." So not what he wanted to be talking about right now.

"Okay."

"Karen." He tipped her chin up until her gaze met his. "I love you."

She shivered, and he lifted her hand, laying a row of small kisses across her knuckles. "I've only said that to one other woman. Plus my mother. And Meg. And I've never felt it quite like this before, so you gotta know, all joking aside, I'm not sneaking you into my room. You belong here."

A lone tear rolled down her cheek, and he moved his lips to capture it.

"Don't cry, baby."

"I don't know—"

"You don't need to know. I do. I promise."

"There's so much to talk about." She ran her hands over his chest. "And that's hard to do when you say beautiful things and look...beautiful in front of me."

"Lower." He glanced down at her hands. "Touch me."

"Maybe we shouldn't confuse the issue."

He took her hands and helped her push down his shorts. "This isn't confusing anything. This is putting the truth of us front and center. How good we are together. How much we want each other." As if on command, his dick, already hard and panting for her touch, bobbed up and down.

"It's just sex," she whispered, her shaky fingers wrapping around his erection.

Instead of arguing, he surged his hips forward, pumping his cock through her grip a few times. Need unfurled in his gut and he sank to his knees, taking her shorts to the ground at the same time. Her scent swirled toward him, delicate and musky and intoxicating, and he buried his face in the warm soft skin above her mound. She stroked his head, and he nuzzled her belly before tilting his face up to look at her beautiful face. Eyes still wide. Lips still parted in disbelief. "This isn't sex, Karen. This is love."

With gentle precision, he eased her hips back against the bed, and lifted one leg, draping it over his shoulder as he reached between them to part her sex, both of them groaning quietly as his touch found her wet and ready. As he dipped his face and kissed her clit, he felt her lean back, bracing herself against the bed, and he pressed her knee up and away, revealing more of her lusciousness.

He was drunk on her taste. With each lick, his mind swirled faster and harder, and his dick pulsed between his legs, wanting to be inside her. As she trembled and shook, grinding against his face, he thought about telling her everything. Admitting just how far down their future path he'd imagined.

But he needed to follow her lead now. She had fears, and doubts, and he for all the promises that he wanted to make, that's all they would be. There weren't any guarantees. Hard to believe while on his knees, worshiping the woman he loved, but love wasn't the only truth between them. Distance and responsibility couldn't be ignored. The next year would be a challenge, but they'd get through it together.

Above him, Karen panted his name, and he redoubled his efforts, looping up and around her clit with his tongue, then dipping lower to surge inside, and back again, until one of her hands clamped onto the back of his head and held him in place as she exploded in a jerky, beautiful clench.

He almost pushed her flat on bed and mounted her bare, but at the last second remembered a condom.

It was the last conscious thought he had before he sank into her tight warmth and surrendered to his need.

———

"I HAD a whole thing planned out. It was going to be special, me telling you how I feel."

"This was pretty special." Karen trailed one of the damp washcloths that Paul had brought back from the bathroom over his back. It was hot and sticky, and the fan wasn't quite cutting it. She lazily thought about opening his window, but it was all the way across the room.

"I wanted to ask you out."

"Like on a date? That's adorable." She smirked, and he twisted to the side as if to tickle her, but his palm brushed her nipple and he shifted focus. As he drew tighter and tighter circles on her breast, pebbling the skin and stirring the hungry beast inside her —two crashing orgasms weren't enough?—she fell back against the pillow and arched her back. "Tell me what we were going to do," she panted.

"Maybe I shouldn't tell you. We could still do it."

"We will. But it doesn't need to be a surprise anymore, does it?"

"I guess not." He sucked her nipple into his mouth and hummed before releasing it. "I'd decided to take you hiking up the bluffs. Bring a camera, take a picture of us with the town and the lake below."

Her heart skipped a beat. "Wow."

"We can still do that."

"You better believe it." She should tell him. As he made love to her, the words had echoed in her head, over and over again. *I love you, too.* She did. But again, as an opportunity presented itself, she ducked.

"You okay?"

She nodded.

"Want to come again?"

Another nod. Good lord, she didn't deserve this man.

20

—————

I T took a minute for Karen to realize she was dreaming. She was standing in her kitchen, making a cup of tea, and it wasn't until she blinked and was all of a sudden outside, in the cool darkness of her backyard, that awareness set in. She turned around, trying to get her bearings. The upstairs light was on next door. She looked at her watch, knowing that it was Megan's bedtime even though she couldn't make out the face. Paul would be on his third trip up to tell her to put the books away. Despite her aching heart, Karen couldn't help but laugh out loud, which wasn't out loud at all. Dreams were weird.

Sadness flooded her chest as she looked at their house. She'd been in her own kitchen, and now she was standing on the outside, looking in. What had gone wrong?

She wondered how long it would be before she saw the eerie glow of a secret flashlight, and barked another silent laugh.

"What's so funny?"

She froze. His voice never changed. Years of feigning understanding with criminals had polished his tone into quiet consistency. It was the words itself that did the damage.

"Karen." He stepped closer, his footsteps slow but undaunted by her silence.

"Shouldn't you be telling Megan to turn out her light?"

He chuckled, and the warm rolling sound punched her in the gut. Her dream self started to fill in the gaps. This wasn't tonight, or it was, but an alternate version where they hadn't reconnected. God, she'd missed him, even in her dreams.

"We're trying something new—natural consequences of staying up late. I'm going to haul her out of bed for a hike in the morning."

"There's nothing natural about that," she muttered, and smiled despite herself. It actually sounded amazing. A thermos of coffee and a bag of Carrie's muffins at the top of the moraine would make it perfect.

"I want to talk. About us."

"Haven't we talked enough? You made it crystal clear that you don't feel the same way." Had he? Where did she get that idea from?

"I don't."

Dream Karen waved him off. "Really not necessary to go over that again."

"It is."

Above their heads, Megan's bedroom window went dark. "She's so good, isn't she?" It was reaching, but any subject change would work. But Karen didn't know why she was changing the subject. *Go back,* she wanted to scream at her dream self. *Let him talk, it'll be worth it.*

He nodded.

"You guys have done a great job raising her." Her dream heart squeezed, and then she was inside herself, losing her objective view of the scene, and the pain was hot and real. "I'm really glad that it's okay with you and Susan that Megan still hangs out with me." Her voice grew tight and cold, and she hated it, but there was a limit to how polite she could be. "I'm going inside no—"

"Stop." Again with that damn cop voice. How did he manage to make a request sound like an order, and an order sound like a plea? Reading true desperation into his unchanged tone would surely make her the pathetic one.

She halted anyway, but only to lob one last volley. "You don't get any more of my time, Paul. Fool me once, ya know?"

Standing taller than she felt, she headed inside. He was following, but she knew he wouldn't enter her house uninvited. Despite the late fall chill, a faint sweat burst across her upper body. If she could just close the slider door without turning around, before he said—

"I love you."

It was as if she knew it was coming, and yet was blindsided anyway. Like a lift hill at the start of a roller coaster. Of course he loved her. She'd known that from their first kiss. Probably from their first late night conversation in this very yard. But he didn't love her like she loved him. He didn't *want* to love her. That's why he pushed her away. And since he was able to push her away, able to hurt her so readily, with such ease, he couldn't love her as he should. As she deserved. He'd found some of the words to describe how he felt, but they were too little, too late.

There was only one thing she could do. Protect her heart. Lie. "I don't care."

"Please, let me explain."

She was still standing with her back to him. She wanted to turn around, wanted to sink into his arms and his words and let him make it okay, but it wasn't going to be okay. They didn't want the same things in life. There was no future, and she wasn't going to waste any more time pretending that there just might be.

With a gasp, she woke up just as she headed away from Paul in her dream, and twisted into Paul in real life. She was in his bed, their naked bodies entwined in a sticky pile. And he loved her. For real. But also in a dream where they hadn't been talking. Oh, god.

He'd told her he loved her, and she'd said nothing.

She had to go.

———

LUNCHTIME. He could stop at the store, pick something up, visit the woman he loved, even when she drove him out of his mind with equal parts desire and concern. She'd snuck out of his place while he was asleep two nights ago, and blown him off when he asked her about it the next day. She'd visited for a bit that same afternoon, played a few rounds of Wii Sports, but then headed into the city to see her sister and she wasn't home when he went to bed.

Just because he'd said he loved her didn't mean she had to spend every night in his bed. Yeah, right. Maybe if he repeated that to himself enough times he'd believe it.

A bell jangled overhead as he pushed the door open. Underfoot, the soft cream linoleum was worn, but clean and recently waxed. A cheerful greeting drifted his way from the cashier, and he nodded, but his gaze kept moving. Cataloguing the space without thinking about it. Tidy, full shelves. Sale signs, bright and in his face. A few mid-day customers, moving slowly, none of them taking notice of him. He'd become a part of the town. Constable Reynolds of the Wardham Detachment, seen at the grocery store picking up lunch. No longer a source of gossip. That would change shortly.

"Excuse me, miss?" The clerk glanced up. "Karen around?"

She pointed to the back corner of the store. "I think she's stocking in aisle six."

He heard her humming before he rounded the corner. Guns N' Roses. Ha. He paused, giving himself a moment to soak in the goodness.

Her hair was piled on her head in a cross between a ponytail and a bun, and as she stretched to stack cracker boxes on the top shelf, an inviting curve of bare tummy revealed itself between her jeans and cotton t-shirt. She looked determined, if tired, and a renewed desire to ease her burden coursed through his gut.

But she wasn't making that easy for him to do. "You were out late last night."

She froze in place, one long arm stretched above her head. He moved closer, stopping as he picked up her familiar tropical-tinged scent. Another foot and he wouldn't be able to maintain any distance between them at all. Even here, safely just out of arm's reach, every fiber of his being was humming with a need to touch her. Protect her. Consume her, which probably ran counter to the protection instinct.

"So?" She pushed off the shelf and turned toward him, her chest rising and falling slowly as she controlled her breath. He waited for her to cross her arms, or prop her hands on the tight waist he desperately wanted to stroke his own hands around. But instead she reached up to rub the skin at the base of her neck, and his gaze was drawn to the pink flush there.

"So nothing, just noticed is all." Notching his hands on his belt, he relaxed his arms in a gesture he hoped conveyed all that he couldn't say in a busy grocery store. *Am I messing this up? I don't want to be needy, I just want you. All the time. Because we don't have that much time.*

She closed her eyes for a moment, then opened them and offered a rueful smile. "I don't know why I didn't call you. I'm glad to see you now."

"It's okay that I stopped by?" He risked her siren call in the name of privacy and stepped closer. "I came to ask you out."

A laugh was not the response he'd expected, but the throaty outburst wasn't the worst answer she could have given. "Hiking?"

"Yep."

"Okay." She leaned forward, so their heads were mere inches apart. Her breath was warm and sweet, like she'd been chewing fruity gum. "I really am glad to see you today."

He reached out and twirled an errant curl with his index finger before carefully tucking it behind her ear, an excellent excuse to touch her skin. He lingered there for a moment before trailing his fingertips along her jaw. When he reached her chin, he paused, then regretfully withdrew his hand.

Low enough to keep his words just for her, he opened his heart and let the truth out. "I'm not going give you a lot of space, unless you tell me to back off. I'd rather spend the next two months getting my fill of you than pretending that being apart is easier, because it's not. Being apart from you is hell on earth."

Her eyes widened and her lips parted. Good, she hadn't expected that. He grinned.

"Your fill of me?" She pursed her lips and narrowed her eyes. "Is that a good thing?"

"I promise, I'll make it good." He saw her retort coming and kept talking. "Good enough to last you through months of scholastic-induced celibacy."

Another laugh. "I'll come home for visits."

They both knew that wouldn't be enough. But that was a conversation for a more private time and place.

"You want to come over tonight? I told Megan you might be sleeping over, so you wouldn't need to sneak out again."

She looked chagrined. "I woke up around five and thought it might be best…"

"Baby, it's fine. I just missed you."

"K. I've got a girls' night tonight, but maybe after that?"

"Will you be tipsy?"

"Probably." Her gaze flicked down his body, moving left to right in a zigzag pattern, taking stock of him with honest hunger that gave him a decent boner before he could get control of his physical reaction.

Fine. Two could play at that game. "Good. Wear that skirt we never got around to violating the other day."

She swallowed what sounded suspiciously like a moan, and he took a quick step back before his dick took over and he molested her in the cracker aisle.

It wasn't exactly smooth, or romantic, but it would do. "Karen?"

She took a deep breath before responding. "Yeah?"

"I'm going to get better at this."

21

———

H^E was already better than anyone else who'd ever been interested in her. A short list, sure, but he still topped the list in a major way.

Mari had offered her kid-free apartment for the girls' night, which was conveniently just down the street from the store, so Karen sent Melody home a bit early and locked up herself. She was the first to arrive, but Carrie and Stella came together a few minutes later. Cousins by marriage, the two women were total opposites, but thick as thieves. Carrie was bubbly and outgoing, a vivacious, curvy woman with bright red Manic Panic hair and what looked like a brand new nose piercing. Karen didn't understand what her friend liked about piercings, but at a previous girls' night, she'd admitted to having her nipples pierced before she had kids. Whatever floated her boat.

Stella, on the other hand, wore a plain blue t-shirt and blue jeans. Everything about her screamed natural, from her own red hair, more strawberry blond than red, long and fine and twisted in a braid down her back, to her scrubbed clean face and serious demeanor. The two women shared a passion for Wardham, and spent a lot of time working together on furthering projects that would raise the town's profile as a tourist destination. Stella lived on the Nixon family's maple syrup farm, and Karen knew she was trying to convince her father and uncle they should do a big festival the following winter.

Laney and Evie were the last to arrive, and by the time they knocked on the door of Mari's apartment, the margaritas were flowing and the bowl of salsa had already been replenished once.

Karen gave Laney a big hug and apologized for missing her engagement party, which Laney waved off and immediately shifted the conversation to Chase's care. They weren't close friends, but over the last six months, Karen had really come to admire Laney; for her career, and for taking a big leap of faith in re-starting her relationship with her first love, Kyle.

"So the latest news is that he's going to start rehab next week. He had a new set of x-rays today, and they're happy with every-thing, so he's got more permanent fiberglass casts on now, which will be easier to wash around, and lighter to move with. His right leg, he might actually be able to bear weight on soon, does that make sense?"

"He doesn't have a rod in that leg?"

Karen shook her head. "I don't think so, but it has a cast."

"The cast might be as much for pain management as letting the fractures heal. Keeping the leg immobilized is more effective than pain killers, even. So if they say that he can toe-touch, that's great. It'll make getting in and out of the wheelchair easier, and in a couple more weeks, if that cast comes off, switch to crutches."

"Hopefully he's on crutches by the time he comes home."

Evie drifted over, a full margarita in her hand, which she set on the coffee table. "He's not going to Phoenix?"

Karen shook her head. "He's adamant that his rehab is here. Ridgemount Nursing Home has a pool, and an accessible apart-ment that he could rent for the first little while. I don't understand why he's leaving Phoenix. It's like he's already given up on hockey, but the team hasn't given up on him."

"It's a normal reaction to trauma, but it can be quite confusing from the outside looking in." Laney set her glass on the coffee table, and after a beat, picked up Evie's and started drinking it. Karen glanced over at Evie, but her friend was staring off into the distance and didn't seem to notice. Audrey would bitch-slap her if she stole her sister's drink, but maybe Evie was driving. Also, Audrey was a spitfire. Karen grinned at the thought and went for a refill of her own.

Carrie found her in the kitchen. "So…spill."

"About what?" Karen gave her a good, long side-eye glance and took a deep breath. "Okay. We should go sit."

"Not good?"

"No, good." A nervous flutter danced through her chest. "Very good. Just confusing."

Carrie pushed her back into the living room and everyone settled down. Karen felt a bit on display, but she needed advice, and the more the better.

"Paul told me he loves me." She glanced around the room, taking in the positive expressions of her friends. "And I didn't say it back." They just waited. "Well? What does that mean?"

Carrie was the first to speak. "We don't know. You tell us."

"I don't know either! I mean, of course I love him. He's…you know?"

Carrie shook her head. "No, not really."

Karen took a fortifying drink. It didn't do anything for the growing-ever-louder pulse she could feel at the base of her neck and hear behind her ears, a staccato drum beat for the thoughts she was afraid to voice out loud. "He's my everything. And I want him, but I want to go to school, and stay in school this time, and not come running back to him because I'm a pathetic, love-drunk fool."

Understanding dawned around her, and one by one, they each shared an anecdote about surprising themselves with tenacity, or courage, or trust. Laney was the last to speak, and for a minute, Karen wasn't sure she would. But of everyone, she suspected that Laney could most closely identify with her dilemma.

"You know that Kyle and I have been doing the long-distance thing for the last six months."

She did—the whole town knew when Kyle was heading to Chicago for a weekend, or when Laney would be visiting Wardham. There was an analogy to be made there about Laney being the sun and Kyle having different climates, but Karen was tipsy and the precise imagery eluded her. Suffice it to say, it was frosty when they were apart. "It seems like it's been hard, to be honest."

"Yep, I won't lie. I'm really looking forward to moving into our new house together, and our little family being whole again."

"New house?"

Laney ruefully nodded her head. "Kyle's had enough of getting up with Buddy and heading down an elevator and a few blocks away to the park at six in the morning. Can't say I blame him. Besides, my condo is convenient, but it was never home. We found a fixer-upper that Kyle can put his mark on."

"Wow, congratulations." She meant it, but envy still tinged her words.

Laney looked like she understood. "It's sweeter for having waited, though. I mean, don't get me wrong, I'm sure I'd be ecstatic if our path to being together had been easier, but our time apart didn't weaken the core of what we have. Every weekend together was concentrated, and special. I'll always remember my drives back and forth fondly."

"And the time between visits? Working and missing him…"

"Evie told me about how you left this program once before." Karen blushed, but Laney wasn't passing judgment. "You're a different person now. You've got a goal, and it sounds like a really supportive guy. Only time will tell, but for me, I actually found throwing myself into work helped the weeks go by faster between visits. I became super productive, knowing I'd want two weekends a month clear and free—for the most part. Sometimes I had to work while we were together, but so did he. That's life, even for couples who aren't geographically separated."

"Totally. When I was starting the bakery, I swear the only time

Ian and I saw each other was Saturday night family dinner and brunch on Sunday morning. The rest of the time we were two ships passing in the night for months on end. Same for our kids; they spent a lot of time with their grandparents that spring." Carrie sighed at the memory. "More than once, I wondered if I was making a giant mistake."

"You never said anything," said Karen.

"Same reason you hesitated to share about your worries about Paul, maybe. Didn't want to voice the fear, in case that became an excuse to give up."

Karen's face turned red. There was her fear, laid out in the open.

"One difference between now and back then, this time you've got Paul firmly on your side." Carrie winced. "Your parents rock, but they're a little too nice, ya know? Maybe they should have kicked your ass and sent you back to school."

She hadn't thought about it like that. A protest had germinated deep in her gut, but that was rooted in loyalty. Carrie wasn't wrong.

"Is it too trite to offer that everything happens for a reason, and leave it at that?" Mari gestured to the kitchen. "There are more margaritas to be had!"

The next hour was spent catching up on gossip. About the slow as molasses plans for the community centre—

"Karen, at this rate, you'll be done school before construction on the new library even begins!"

—and a mysterious new store that was going in on the corner of Watson and Heritage—

"The windows were papered over last week and no one knows who the holding company is leasing it to…"

—to the regular rumours about the West brothers and their playboy ways.

"I heard that Ty is getting serious about someone for the first time ever." Mari leaned forward and splayed her hands out for effect. "And he's been in for lunch with the same woman three times in the last two weeks. They looked cozy. And he hasn't been in at night, flirtin' it up as per usual. This rumour might be true."

Stella snorted.

"What?"

"Never going to happen."

Carrie nodded her head in agreement. "Gotta go with Stella on this one. He's going to be a bachelor forever. Evan has a greater chance of settling down than his brother does."

Evie, who had been quiet and withdrawn to that point, laughed under her breath. "That'll never happen, either."

Karen knew Evie had dated the older West brother in high school, but the younger women probably didn't. It was a good thing they didn't end up together. Evie and Evan. Ugh.

"Why?" Carrie asked the question they were all thinking. Evie pressed her lips together and shook her head, but a rousing protest rose around the room and she tossed her head back and sighed.

Evie gave each of them a serious look before taking a deep breath—and blushing. "It's not a secret that Evan's gay, and it's not a secret that we dated for a couple of years. We were happy, and…suffice it to say that being with me wasn't a problem for him." She glanced around the room again, and Karen only saw interest, no judgment. Her own pulse picked up a bit, wondering what was coming next. "This isn't inside knowledge at all, but my guess is, the type of relationship that would finally hook Evan isn't with one other person."

Wow.

"What other kind of relationship is there?" Stella wrinkled her brow, then looked affronted when Laney and Carrie burst into hysterical laughter on either side of her.

"Oh honey, you need to spend a little less time reading your textbooks and pick up a ménage romance novel instead." Carrie sighed. "I'd like a second husband from time to time."

"Would Ian go for that?" Laney looked almost hopeful. Karen

made a mental note to add a few books to her own reading list as well, it sounded like she was missing out.

"Not a chance in hell."

"Threesomes are intense, that's for sure." Evie turned beet red as everyone swivelled their heads back to her again.

Karen blinked hard, processing what her friend had just shared. "Evie! You and the guy in Toronto?"

Carrie gasped and wagged her finger in the air. Only Laney remained un-fazed.

"No, not the guy in Toronto." She shook her head. "Evan. A long time ago, and it wasn't my scene. But it meant something to him, more than just hot sex."

"Wow." Karen finally found her voice. "Look at what comes out when we ban the men and add a bit of tequila."

———

THE SHORT WALK home from Mari's apartment above Danny's took a bit longer when tipsy, but between wondering what was going on with Evie, who had been distracted all night before dropping the mega bomb of sharing, and thinking about Carrie's typically acerbic analysis of her family relations, she was at her driveway before she knew it, and had to double back a few feet. Before she made it to her porch, Paul's front light switched on.

Even better. His bed was bigger. His cock was yummier. She snorted and smacked her hand over her mouth. *Keep it together, his daughter is in there, too.*

His front door swung open, and pure bliss coursed through her veins as she took in the glorious sight of her favourite half-naked man, wearing nothing but a pair of sweatpants that sat low on his lean hips.

Paul raised his eyebrows, silently repeating the same question she'd just asked herself, when she leaned happily against his door frame and waved her hands up and down in front of his bare torso. "This is very nice, sir."

He grunted, and tugged her inside. "I could get used to hearing you call me that."

"Yes, sir!" She jerked to attention, but nearly toppled in the opposite direction as she over-compensated for the movement.

"Come on, darlin', let's get you to bed."

"Naked bed?"

"Sleeping bed."

"You can take advantage of me, sir, I don't mind."

"I do."

"Hey!" They were halfway up the stairs, but she didn't care. Megan was probably sleeping, so she kept her voice low, but a protest could still be made. She twisted, taking care to hang on to the bannister because doing a header back down the stairs would be a terrible idea, and plunked her butt down on the soft carpet running up the center of the staircase. That was when she noticed she was still wearing her shoes. Flipping them one at a time down the stairs bought her a bit of time to think ever so carefully about what she wanted to say next. The wine might have muddled her head a bit, but logic was on her side for this point. "I stumble home, you flip on your light, I don't need to ask what that means. We might not have had our first official date yet, but I think we're past the point of you needing to worry if I'm sober or not."

He tucked in behind her and squeezed her neck before working to release her hair from its ponytail. He sucked in a breath, then held it, as if he stopped himself from saying something. After a minute, he started again, and this time kept going. "You're probably right. It's a thing for me."

"A big deal thing or a little deal thing?" Unexpected worry started to nibble at her gut. Was this part of why he thought he wasn't a good guy? Crappity crap. She should be sober for that conversation.

"Just a little deal thing, I promise."

"I don't get it." Confusion warred with desire—for him, not just in this moment, but for always. Whatever issues he'd had in the past, did they really matter? He'd proven over and over again that the Paul of here and now was good and decent. And hot. "You really don't want to sleep with me tonight?"

"Sleep, yes. Want to do more, yes. But it's…" He growled quietly as he leaned forward and kissed the top of her head. "Why won't you just let me tuck you in like a good girl?"

"Because I've learned it's so much more fun to be bad."

"Just what did you ladies talk about tonight?"

Karen giggled quietly to herself. Should she share?

His hand pulsed against her neck. "Maybe I should give you a sobriety test."

"What do I get if I pass?"

"An orgasm or two."

Hot diggity. "Lead the way."

22

———

"KAREN, are you awake?"

Under the light summer weight blanket she must have yanked over her head to block out the morning sun, Karen froze. Sun. Morning. *Crappity crap.*

A quick head-to-toe check reassured her she was decently attired, so she slowly peeled back the covers enough to show her face and offer a brave smile to Paul's daughter, standing in the open bedroom doorway. "I sure am!"

"I brought you a cup of coffee." Megan came in and set a steaming mug on the bedside table. "Dad said we should let you sleep in, but I'm too excited about the hike."

"Right." Karen glanced around the room, but Paul must have tidied at some point. No evidence of anything inappropriate, except for her in his bed. Wearing his t-shirt and what felt like a pair of his boxer shorts. Maybe she'd leave the covers on until Megan left the room.

"Are you okay?"

No. "Yep!"

"You look kinda freaked out."

She needed more prep for a conversation like this. "Why don't you head downstairs and I'll be along in a jiffy, okay?"

Megan shrugged and headed for the stairs, shouting back over her shoulder, "Breakfast is almost ready!"

Downstairs, she found Paul watching over a skillet of pancakes and sausages, holding a matching mug to hers. She smoothed her sundress over her hips, grateful Megan hadn't seen it the day before. She'd need to go home for a quick shower and more hiking appropriate clothes, but her stomach told her she should stay for breakfast first.

"Hey." He pulled her close, really close, tucking his arm around her like this wasn't a totally weird situation.

"We need to talk," she said quietly, hoping that the lack of volume wouldn't keep the urgency from getting through.

From his raised eyebrow response, that wasn't a problem. "About what?"

"Megan waking me up? All of a sudden you just being okay with all of this?"

"You're freaking out."

"Yes!" She pressed her free hand, the one not pinned tight to his side, to her chest and rubbed a tight circle there. "We've just went from zero to sixty in, like, five seconds."

"Baby." Damn him and his calm voice that cut through her anxiety and made her feel all warm and melty. "What can I do to make this less weird?"

"I don't know. Maybe I just need some time."

"Hmmm. Time doesn't really work for me, since we've already wasted a good deal, and don't have much left before you head to Toronto."

"I know, but—" She squirmed against his side, taking advantage of him leaning forward to flip pancakes to move away, but his other hand reached out and snagged her wrist, pulling her back against him. "Stop that."

"No." He set the spatula down and crowded her against the counter, caging her in with his legs, set wide on either side of hers, and his arms, which bracketed her body. Tan, corded arms, dusted with hair, good enough to eat…*Damn*. Now she was turned on and pissed off. And his daughter was somewhere in the house.

"Paul, you're overwhelming me."

He stilled for a moment, then kissed her, a gentle, restrained reminder of his love. His lips grazed hers, then pressed delicately first on one side of her mouth, then the other. "I'm sorry?"

That did it. That quirky, not-sorry-at-all, cocky-as-all-hell, but also sweet-as-sugar non-apology cut through her panic and made her laugh. "You're not! God, Paul, my head is spinning."

"Low blood sugar. We'll eat some breakfast, then we can talk on the hike."

"I think we need a bit more privacy…and shouldn't we have talked about everything before Megan found me in your bed?"

He smirked at her. "I made sure you were decent. She knew you were here, I told her yesterday you'd be sleeping over."

"But I didn't know yesterday that I'd be sleeping over!"

"And yet you're here. In my kitchen, about to eat my pancakes and turkey sausage, so…"

She mock-growled as he stepped away, gesturing widely with his hand as if to say it was her choice to stay or go.

She sat at the table.

He laughed.

She smiled, but waited until he turned back to the skillet.

———

PAUL'S PLAN for privacy on the hike became obvious when they stopped at Evie's house on their way to the bluffs and picked up her kids. Connor and Max recognized Paul from a safety presentation he did at their school, and Evie, who looked uncharacteristically tired, repeatedly thanked them for extending the invitation to her boys.

After expertly organizing all three kids across the backseat, Max in his booster seat, and Megan in the middle, each of their backpacks stashed neatly at their feet, Paul merrily navigated to the conservation area parking lot, going over the Hiker's Code on the way.

Karen was pretty sure he made it up on the spot, but he got immediate buy-in from the kids for always walking with a buddy, staying on the agreed upon marked trails, and doing frequent radio checks. *Radio checks?*

As they piled out of the car and Paul distributed a small Cobra handset to each kid, then handed one to Karen and clipped his own to his belt, she got it.

The kids took off ahead of them, hollering something about snacks at the first check point. Paul shot her a grin, and she laughed.

"Okay, I get it. We'll have all the privacy we need to talk."

"You could add 'sir' to that admission," he teased.

"Not a chance in hell. My inner submissive only comes out when I'm drunk."

"I'll keep that in mind for when I want to spank you." He left her gaping at him as he circled the car to grab his own backpack, then laced his fingers into hers and tugged her toward the trailhead. "Come on, we've given them enough of a headstart."

———

Neither of them broke the comfortable silence until after the first water break with the kids. They were halfway to Paul's mysterious destination, which Megan was apparently familiar with, because she scampered ahead with the boys. The trail climbed steadily, with regular wide plateaus that offered glimpses of the lake through the trees, and now that the opportunity had arrived, discussing the mess of the next year was the last thing Karen wanted.

So of course, Paul slowed his pace. "Okay, let's talk."

"And ruin our first date? Maybe later."

"It won't ruin anything."

"You're sure of yourself."

Ahead of her, he stopped. His technical t-shirt, stretched tight across his broad shoulders, was dotted with sweat, and when he pulled off his pack and set it against a log, she could see a line straight down to his narrow hips.

On her, the sweaty t-shirt look was probably a mess. On him, it smacked of virility and health.

He turned to face her, and set his hands on his hips. He paused a beat, as if carefully considering what to say. "I'm sure of us."

"Wow."

"Is that a good wow?"

"Maybe. Yes." She stared up the trail. When he said it like that, it all seemed so simple. When she looked at him, radiating confidence, she couldn't remember why it wasn't. "Why aren't you scared?"

He shook his head slightly. "I'm scared."

"Not about us."

"Not anymore."

"What are you scared about now?"

"A whole bunch of stuff that isn't first date conversation material." He grinned, this time more rueful than confident. "I'm scared I'm pushing you too hard. That we're not going to get past the first date. That my spanking joke turned you off. That you'll get a job on the other side of the province."

"I'm coming back."

"You better. It'll be embarrassing if I show up somewhere and drag you off, caveman-style."

She moved closer, wanting to touch him. She drifted her hands across his chest, feeling his nipples bead under his shirt. Licking her lips, she lowered her voice. "The spanking thing…that was just a joke?"

His eyes dilated. "That's up to you."

An image of them wrestling popped into her head. It would

start playfully, but progress to pinning each other to the bed, grinding and teasing, and then all of a sudden he'd flip her onto his lap. He'd start with a few swats on top of her shorts, but she'd respond, and at her first moan, he'd wrench her shorts down and smooth his hand over her bare bottom.

Heat flooded her core and her cheeks at the same time. Holy hell, she wasn't ready to ask him to spank her. Instead, she laced her arms around his neck and kissed him until he couldn't help but be clear on how she felt about that prospect.

"Okay, glad we cleared that up." He chuckled quietly against her cheek, smoothing his hand up and down her back. "What are you scared of?"

"Being torn between two places. Not giving school my all. Neglecting you and whatever this is between us."

"Stop saying that." He rolled his shoulders, as if squaring off for a fight. "'Whatever this is.' This is a relationship. I'm your boyfriend. In six weeks, you're going to go away for a while, and I'll be your long-distance boyfriend. When you come home on weekends, each visit will further our relationship a little bit, and at some point, I'll stop being your boyfriend and just be your significant other. In a permanent way."

"My significant other." It didn't quite have the ring of fiancé or husband, but it was the right sentiment. Why did it leave her unsettled?

"Yeah."

"What does that mean?"

"We're kind of getting ahead of ourselves here. Maybe we could agree this is actually a relationship before debating what to call the next stage?"

"No!" She shouted the word, all of a sudden shaking with emotion. "That's the problem. That's why I said, 'whatever this is.' I don't know what that means. I don't know where you see us a few months, a year, five years from now. I'm scared that we don't want the same things. I'm pretty sure that I want to be more than someone's *significant other.*"

"What the hell do you think I mean? I love you, Karen!" He wasn't yelling exactly, but an uncharacteristic frustration crept into Paul's voice.

"Yeah, well, I love you, too, but that doesn't mean—" Paul held up his hand and Karen froze.

"You love me?"

She nodded.

"Baby."

"What?"

"Shut up, that's what." With ease, he swept her off the ground and kissed her hard and deep, his tongue gliding hungrily into her mouth. As she slid down his body and found terra firma again with her toes, he pinned her tight against him, where she could feel his cock growing with interest. "You love me?"

"Of course I do." She licked her lips, part nervous energy, part appreciation for the kiss they just shared.

"And you're scared." He shook his head. "Shit, I've bungled this." He kicked his backpack out of the way and pulled them down to sit side-by-side on the log. "When I said significant other, I meant, whatever you want us to be. Every time you come home, we're going to lie awake in bed and talk about the future, and I'm going to get little clues about you, and hopefully if you want something straight up, you'll come out and tell me. And I'll do the same. No limits here. I'm not saying I don't want to marry you, I just saying that's your choice."

"Okay." She wanted to say more, but her head was swimming and even though they were sitting, she thought it might be possible that she'd pass out.

"You want to talk about any of that now?"

She shook her head. She really liked the idea of it coming out gradually over time.

"Can I share something that I want?"

"Of course." Relief so sharp she could taste it was rolling through her body. A future they would craft together. Holy crap.

He tugged her hand, pulling her up and onto his lap, holding her hips steady as she straddled him. "One of these days, I want to talk about ditching the condoms." Between them, his arousal was in full-force. On her hips, his grip tightened. "This is so the wrong place for this conversation, I know, but…"

"No, it's okay. I'll look into my options."

"Something not too long term, maybe."

It took a moment for his meaning to sink in. Oh. OH. "Yeah?" First she was going to pass out, now she was pretty sure she was going to hyperventilate.

"Would that be okay with you?" His hold on her shifted, his left hand drifting to the small of her back, his right hand coming around, up and under her shirt, to rest on the softness of her belly. Her sex clenched at the thought of taking him inside her, no barrier, and conceiving a child. "I know this is crazy outside the first date zone, but…"

"We'd have to wait until after I start school, and figure out when would be a good time to take a break. But as long as I get my course work done and out of the way…" She leaned forward and gently bit his bottom lip.

"Yeah?" He tipped his head back and howled. How he'd ever gotten so lucky, he'd never figure it out. He didn't deserve this woman, perched on his lap, willing to give him the world. Hot damn.

"We have to catch up with the kids, who knows what trouble they've gotten into, but this is a conversation I want to have again, and again."

"Yeah? It's not creepy?" He grinned and pressed a hard, quick kiss on her lips before shifting her backwards with regret. They both glanced at his erection. It was a shame to let that go to waste, but… "On we go. I just need a minute."

Karen crossed her arms to keep herself from reaching out to him again. Every fibre of her being was vibrating with love and happiness.

"You standing there, pressing your breasts together like that…

it's not helping, ya know?" He groaned as she turned away and before she knew it, his hard body was pressed against her back-side. "I like that view just as much. Come on. I'll think of math, or something."

———

WHEN THEY REACHED the lookout point, they found the kids relaxing under a tree, eating apples. He dumped his pack next to them and pulled out the sack of peanut butter sandwiches. Karen, though, went straight to the line of boulders that framed the reason why he'd chosen this trail.

"Oh, wow. How did you find this? I've lived here my whole life and I had no idea this view was at the top of these trails." Below them, green treetops tumbled down a ravine, on the other side of which was the lighthouse point, and to the right stretched the town of Wardham, a neat packet of houses on a grid of right-angled streets, dotted here and there with parks and commercial strips. In front of it, along the lake, the public beach, with Lake Erie glittering with the reflection of the mid-day sun.

"Martinez told me. As soon as I saw it, I thought of you." He lightly rested his hand on her hip, tugging her close without inter-rupting her awe.

"Seriously, Paul. I'm just..." She pressed her hand against her chest like she was trying to keep her excitement inside and turned her shining face to look straight at him. "This is the best first date. You were right, this is perfect."

He grinned. "Time for our picture?"

"Wait." She took both of his hands in hers and squeezed, sending bolts of anticipation up his arms and straight to his heart. "I love you." She closed her eyes and smiled, then repeated the words, pausing between one. "I. Love. You."

"You're not just saying that again because I blew your mind with the view?" He was mostly teasing, but needed to be sure.

"Nuh-uh. When I think of how many different ways we could've not ended up here…I want you to know without a doubt how much I love and appreciate you."

"Now you're just spoiling me." He kissed her forehead and pulled out his phone to take a picture.

EPILOGUE

S HE'D fallen asleep. He didn't mind, at all, but she wanted to go home.

Not to her room twenty feet away, now occupied by her tenants, and not to his room upstairs, which his inner caveman wanted to drag her up to and never let her out. She wanted to go back to her parents', where she'd officially moved her stuff at the beginning of August.

Unofficially, half her shit was upstairs. Where it belonged.

"My mom hasn't slept through the night in a week, it's like Chase is a freakin' newborn or something. I don't have to do anything tomorrow, so I can stay up tonight, give her a break, and then she'll be in a better mood for the weekend." Karen had launched into a rant over dinner about her brother being picky, and rejecting the nursing home accommodation he'd lined up. "It was his freakin' idea in the first place. I don't know why he couldn't stay in Phoenix. Or Windsor, for that matter. My parents' house isn't a rehab facility."

Paul had met Grace Miller a few times over the month of August, and never seen her anywhere approaching a bad mood, but he could imagine that things in the Miller house were getting a bit tense. Chase had been back for almost a month. A week after he returned, the same day that Karen moved out of her house, he decided he wanted to stay at the Miller place after all. Karen was displaced from the main floor guest room, to the loft, which wasn't the end of the world, but it started a chain reaction of little disgruntlements.

He grinned. He shouldn't enjoy profiting from the misfortune of others, but it didn't take long for Karen to start hiding out at his place. She'd slept over more nights than not, and been around for part of the days she still slept away from him.

Life was good.

She shifted in front of him on the couch, and the heavy swell of her breast shifted into the palm of his hand. Life was great. He reached his other arm around her waist, blindly searching for the TV remote.

"Don't change it, I'm watching that."

"Your eyes are closed."

"Resting." She yawned. "It's time for me to go, isn't it?"

"If you want to."

"Hush. It's one night. Audrey will be home for the weekend, so I'll be here every night until I go."

Five more nights until she loaded up the Camaro and headed up the 401 to Toronto, and a year of school. A year away from him. "Listen, I was thinking. When you come home on the weekends, what do you think about coming home…here?"

She glanced at him over her shoulder. "Are you asking me to move in with you?"

"Yeah. Are you saying yes?" He still had her breast in his hand. He stroked his thumb back and forth over her nipple, enjoying the darkening, glazed-over look she was giving him. Her lips parted, and he rolled her underneath him, holding himself up off the couch until her legs parted and he could settle in his happiest place of all, between them. "Say yes."

"I would if I could, but I'm being tortured right now." She panted and arched her back as he bit the tender skin behind her ear.

"I want to know that you're coming home to me, every time."

"I am. I will be." She snaked her hand between them and reached into his jeans. Oh, *holy mother of*—his eyes rolled back in his head as she did something clever with her thumb.

The torturer becomes the tortured. He groaned, and she caught his eye. *Kiss me,* she silently begged, and he did, matching the movement of their mouths to that of her hand, building them both to the point of feverish need. They shucked their clothes and he settled upright on the couch, legs splayed wide, and she rode him until they came together.

"Love you, baby," he whispered into her damp skin.

She kissed his shoulder. "Right back atcha."

———

THE MILLERS' hosted a going away barbeque on the beach across the road from their house three nights later. Paul was surprised at how many people went out of their way to greet him, and offer him casseroles while Karen was away. He refrained from pointing out that he'd been cooking for himself for twenty years, and casseroles weren't really his thing. He figured he might be able to pass them on to Evie Calhoun, who was doing a decent job of hiding her secret, but wouldn't be able to for much longer. He wondered if Karen knew, and if he should have told her. Not his story to share, though. From the constant vigil Liam McIntosh was keeping over the pretty blond, albeit from afar, it looked like Evie wasn't completely alone in her journey. And when the town found out…Paul knew that despite the quiet and sometimes conservative nature of the community, when one of their own was in need, they'd band together.

When he found Karen, a little way down the shore, skipping stones with Megan, he paused and just watched. His women. And Megan was rapidly turning into a woman. They'd celebrated her eleventh birthday the week before, in the city. Karen had tried to beg off, but Susan had called her and the next thing he knew, they were all at the restaurant having a decent time together. Would wonders never cease.

"Come on, we should get back," he heard Karen call, and he felt the moment that she saw him as they turned to come back. The weight of the air between them lifted for a second, as if pushed outward by the force of her smile, and she picked up the pace a bit, tugging Megan along with her.

"You guys hungry?" he asked as they neared. "Rumour has it they've got full-fat sausages on the grill."

"Are you calculating in your head how many extra miles you'd have to run to make them worthwhile?" Karen laughed, and reached for his hand, linking his family together. On the other side of her, Megan started a monologue about the awesomeness of mustard. The way she sold it, he was convinced.

———

SHE COULD HEAR the phone ringing. *Fudgesicle.* The keys slipped through her fingers. Too many deadbolts between her and Paul's voice. Back home, she rarely locked her doors; here, she locked them twice just to go to the basement to do laundry. Once inside, it only took three steps to reach her cell on the bedside table. Studio apartments had some advantages. She rang him back, and he answered immediately.

"Baby." The grin was infectious, even hundreds of kilometers away.

"You rang?"

"I missed you."

"Sorry I'm not coming home this weekend."

"Nope, don't be sorry. You got school work to do, I've got speeding tickets to write."

It was their first weekend apart since she'd moved. And surprisingly, she didn't feel conflicted about it. Miss him, yes. But she had a group project to do, and needed to stay in the city. And his total support made all the difference. Laney had been right on that score.

"Are you going out tonight with your young and single classmates?"

"Nope. I've got a hot date planned later, though. I'm going sit on the dryer and read a chapter on metadata principles." He laughed gently in her ear and she sank back into her pillows. "I bet if you were here, you could help me study."

"Absolutely. Give me a definition."

"Metadata is data that describes data. In other words, it's what we know about stuff."

"Tags and keywords?"

"You've been paying attention."

"I try. So the noises you make during sex that tell me you like what I'm doing?"

She knew where this was going, and flipped open the top button of her jeans. "Mmm-hmmm."

"Yeah, like that." He groaned, and she was reminded of the first time they had phone sex. They'd come so far in a few short months.

"Are you touching yourself?" she whispered.

"Hell, yes."

"Tell me about it."

"You first."

"No, you…"

Her laundry sat for a while before she made it back to the basement.

———

"Baby, you home?"

Her car was parked at the curb, so he knew she was, but he never tired of asking that question.

They'd had five weekends at home like this, one trip to the city, which Megan had loved, and a couple of missed visits between work and school. A comfortable routine had formed, but this weekend was going to be special.

"In the kitchen."

He followed her voice. "You parked on the street."

"I need to run to the liquor store and pick up a bottle of wine."

"I'll go back out if you want." She was chopping vegetables at the counter. His beautiful woman, in his kitchen. Her long legs were covered in denim appropriate for the cooler autumn weather, but the jeans fit snug across her curvy bottom and her fitted t-shirt showed off the nip of her waist and he could imagine how good her—

"You just going to stare at me all afternoon? Come and give me a kiss, mister. I've missed you." She glanced over her shoulder at him and laughed as he covered the space between them before she finished talking. She went back to chopping and he settled in behind her, legs spread wide, arms around her waist, chin on her shoulder.

"You get your paper done?"

"Mmm-hmm. Only have a bit of reading to do this weekend."

"Good, you can do it in bed." It was their first weekend together without Megan, and he was going to soak up as much naked Karen time as he could manage.

"I look forward to it." She set the knife on the counter and elbowed him gently, wanting him out of the way. He grudgingly shifted so she could carry the cutting board to the stove and deposit the chopped carrots and parsnips into what looked like a stew.

"Does that have to simmer for a while?" He couldn't help the hopeful tone in his voice. Didn't really want to, either.

"Mmm-hmm." Karen gave it one last stir and headed for the stairs without looking back at him. She knew he'd follow.

She took her jeans off at the top of the stairs. He'd stop and pick them up. Probably fold them, too. To slow him down even further, she looped her shirt over the bannister. In their room, which now housed two tall wardrobes stuffed to the gills with her clothes, she quickly swapped out her bra and underwear for the silk negligee she'd picked up on Bloor Street. She'd been planning to bring it out later that night, but no time like the present—

The door swung open as she was arranging herself on the bed.

"Hi," she breathed.

His heated gaze took her in. All of her. And got even more heated. "That's pretty."

Gotcha. "I splurged a little."

"I approve." He stripped off his t-shirt and jeans, and her pussy pulsed at the realization that he'd gone commando. Naked and very turned on, her man approached the bed. "You look like an early Christmas present."

She toyed with the ribbon that laced up the front of her torso. "Feel free to unwrap me."

He hovered above her, tracing his fingers across her cheek, down her neck and along the strap of her chemise before tugging, ever so slowly, at the bow she'd offered him. As the lacing loosened, he peeled open the silk, groaning as her erect nipples popped into view. "I miss you during the week," he said, burying his face in her chest.

"Are you talking to me, or them?" She giggled as he surged up to kiss her and scowl.

"Both. Don't ruin this moment I'm having with them." He kissed her again, this time more deeply, reassuring her that he missed every part of her body and mind while she was gone, and while his tongue did its magic, his hands went to work doing theirs, stroking and teasing her body. Somewhere in there, the silk nothing disappeared into actual nothing, and then he was spooning her, ready to enter her from behind.

"Wait!" she gasped. "Are you sure?"

He groaned hard into her hair. "Seriously?"

She swiveled her hips, teasing his swollen head. "No, I mean, I'm sure. I just wanted to check that you…"

He thrust into her, making her gasp again, then moan, as he splayed one hand across her stomach and used the other to fist her hair out of the way. "We talked about this, darlin'. No reason to wait." He moved his hips slowly, pushing deep inside, pulling back just a bit, then surging forward to make contact with her cervix again. "Unless you don't want me to come inside you."

She did. Oh god, she really did. "Please…"

Pushing back, she urged him to pick up the pace, and he did, which set off a chain reaction of physical sensations that ended with what felt like fireworks going off in her brain, her breasts, her sex and every other part of her body all at the same time. As the rest of her being trembled and collapsed, her heart sighed with content.

Behind her, Paul shuddered with an aftershock of his own. "Wow," he said quietly.

"That was worth the hundred dollars I spent on the lingerie, eh?" She sighed.

"That was worth a heck of a lot more than that." He paused. "Except if we're going to have another mouth to feed, maybe not."

She twisted away, stretching out on her stomach, and offered him a languid smile. "It might not take the first time. I only stopped taking the pills this cycle."

"Then we'll keep practicing." He tugged the blanket over her naked body. "You have a catnap, I'll run out for that wine."

THE END

Want more? **Keep reading with** Evie and Liam's unexpectedly perfect love story, and all the other Wardham happy ever afters!

And be sure to read Chase's book, No Time Like Forever. Excerpts of both novels can be found by turning the page!

I ALSO HAVE a mailing list that I use to give readers a heads-up about new releases and big sales. If you sign up, you'll also be given an opportunity to read new releases before they hit stores!

subscribe to my newsletter!
- DEALS
- HOT NAVY SEALS
- QUARTERLY KINDLE GIVEAWAYS
- BE THE FIRST TO HEAR ABOUT
ALL NEW RELEASES!

—Zoe

WHAT TO READ NEXT

WHEN THEY WEREN'T LOOKING (WARDHAM #4)

THE only thing that would make Evie Calhoun's weekend away in the city better would be an orgasm or two. In an ideal world, served up on a platter by a pool boy or a lumberjack.

But even though that wasn't going to happen, she couldn't keep a smile off her face. It had been a near-perfect day, and now she was walking back to her hotel after witnessing a world-class dance performance. A gorgeous lake on one side of her and the city on the other. The sun, setting behind her in the west, lit up the glass towers of Toronto's central business district and what might be an everyday view for others struck her as magical and sophisticated.

No wonder the condos advertised along Lakeshore Drive were so expensive—it was the best of both worlds in one perfect location. Man, what an exciting place to call home.

Evie never would, of course, but she could pretend for a night or two. Her mother had surprised her with a much needed break. Away from Wardham, and her ex-husband, and even her much-loved life with her boys.

Claire Calhoun had given her daughter a train ticket to the city and five hundred dollars, with an order that none of it was to be spent on anything even remotely like a bill or clothes for the kids. Evie was to spoil herself.

And she had: conveyor-belt sushi for dinner the night before, a gorgeous room at the Westin Harbour Castle hotel, a few splurges at Sephora and Victoria's Secret this afternoon, and a front row ticket to see The Mitchell Raz Collective at the Harbourfront Centre.

In another life, Evie might have moved to the city and auditioned for similar companies. Shared a flat uptown with three other girls and bartended all night so she'd be free to dance during the day. But she'd been scared of the odds against her, and her few visits to the city to see Evan in those halcyon early days after graduation had left her underwhelmed. Loud, expensive, dirty. Wardham, with its sleepy beach and zero competition for anything was the more comfortable choice.

And she wouldn't do it any differently, given the chance, because whatever other costs her choices had, she had two beautiful sons who made her world right. Her family, for all the bumps and bruises it had sustained over the last two years, was a wonderful unit. Connor was rapidly turning into a young man, careful and studious, but always staying on the cute side of bossy. Max, two years younger, had finally figured out how to stick a punch-line and used it to maximum advantage in his natural calling as an entertainer. His teacher danced around the term class clown, but grade one had been a hard transition for him, and she expected more of the same in the fall.

But Evie... Somewhere in the mix, she'd let herself be compressed to mother, community member, daughter, and sister. All good, but all giving. This was the first time in years she'd allowed herself to truly indulge. Sleeping in, shopping, dance. She'd joked with her girlfriends about adding sex into the mix, but the closest to that she was going to get this weekend was being able to spread out on the hotel bed and read an erotic romance novel without worrying about hiding it from prying eyes.

Sex.

It had been so long, she might actually have forgotten how to do it.

Two years since she and Dale last made love, although there hadn't been much love in that coupling. Or the infrequent times in the year before that. No love, and even less passion.

Deep down, she yearned for that passion. If she was being honest with herself, what she really wanted was an awesome romp. With someone who didn't lose their erection if she moved in the wrong direction. Someone who wanted her for who she was right now, stretch marks and old lady hands included. Who didn't have a pathetic Madonna/whore complex.

A flash of anger at her ex-husband pulsed through her. She glanced down at her bare fingers, glad to be rid of the rings that hadn't guaranteed the forever they were supposed to.

But she was thirty-five, and a mother, and it had been fifteen years since she'd last had sex for sex's sake. She wouldn't even know where to start in the city, and the thought of actually picking up a stranger…that was an awesome fantasy, and a terrifying reality.

A hot bath and a blush-inducing book would have to be enough.

But first, a drink. Maybe two, because she could sleep in tomorrow.

The hotel bar was empty, but the friendly bartender gestured for her to take a seat. "What can I get you?"

"Something fancy." Wardham's only bar, Danny's, was known for cheap beer and straight shots.

"Do you like peaches?" She nodded, and he began assembling a bellini in front of her. She slid some cash toward him when he finished, and after taking a sip, let her thoughts wander down an imaginary path. If she had come to the city to be a dancer, what would she be doing now? Choreography? Married or single? Still on the audition circuit?

She nursed her drink, lost in a tangled web of what-ifs, and was just about to head upstairs when the bartender placed another bellini in front of her. She shook her head. "Oh, no, I'm sorry, I didn't—"

"It's from the man in the corner," he said.

Evie twisted in her seat to see where he was pointing. Her breath caught in her throat as her gaze collided with dark, unvarnished interest. There were six of them, four men and two women, all in suits, but only one was staring at her like he wanted to eat her up. And as heat sparked in various places throughout her body, being devoured by a perfect stranger suddenly sounded like an excellent idea. Hot damn...

No. What kind of hussy would that make her?

A satisfied one, probably, if he could deliver on the promise in his eyes.

She smiled, enjoying the moment of attention, and nodded her head in thanks. A warm blush crawled up her neck and she spun back to the bar, but a minute later she glanced back over her shoulder. There was something unbelievably tempting about the man. Long and lean, with dark hair and refined features. Quietly handsome, but overtly sexy. Urbane and sophisticated, like he wouldn't blink to discover her Brazilian bikini wax. Like he'd understand the implicit request of it, and dive in for a feast.

It didn't take him long to make his way over to her.

"Can I join you?" His voice was rich and warm with a shiver-inducing edge, like chocolate syrup on vanilla ice cream. Up close he was younger than she first thought. Definitely younger than her, and not just by a few months.

"I suppose it's the least I can do, since you bought me a drink." She glanced up at him from under her eye lashes. God, she had no clue how to flirt. She didn't want to lead him on, but every fibre of her being wanted him to keep talking.

Instead of sitting, he leaned sideways against the bar. "That's not a ringing invitation, but I'll take it." He flashed a crooked smile, the left side of his face curling up in a wink, and butterflies took flight from the pit of her stomach.

"I'm out of practice, I promise it's not personal. I'm Evie." She held out her hand, and something bright sparked in his eyes. Everything around them faded to nothing as he wrapped his hand around hers and she swallowed hard against something that felt suspiciously like a giggle trying to fly out of her mouth.

"Liam." Another smile, and her panties started peeling themselves down her hips. "And I don't have a ton of practice at this either."

"I find that really hard to believe," she admitted, kicking herself momentarily for the honesty, but he just chuckled.

"Where are you from?"

"Out of town." He lifted one eyebrow at the coy response, and a warmth spilled across her chest. This was fun.

"Would you like to join us?" He nodded his head toward his friends. "We've just written our final exams—" A dull roar filled her ears, and her face must have fallen, because he leaned in and touched her forearm. "You okay?"

"Exams?" Her voice came out as a squeak. Holy shit, he was a college student. An incredibly mature, sexy, masculine…kid. She narrowed her eyes at him, then glanced over to his friends. None of them looked like teenagers. Maybe they were grad students. But still.

"Business school. Two years of grueling hell completed. We're heading up to Koreatown next for some karaoke."

Business school. Not babies, just…younger than her. A fun kind of young. Yeah, she could still do this. "Sounds intriguing."

He laughed at the obvious doubt in her voice. "It is, I promise."

Something about the dip in his voice, the private pause, made her come undone, and the giggle snuck out, followed by another. He raised his eyebrows, but he didn't seem concerned by her bizarre behaviour, just amused. "And just how can I trust your judgment on such matters?"

He leaned in close enough for his cologne to faintly imprint on her senses. He smelled yummy and expensive and not really too young at all. She was clearly drunk, which would explain why she licked her lips and tilted her head just so, a move he definitely didn't miss. He paused a few inches away from her face, naked appreciation zinging between them, then shifted his approach and brushed his lips against her ear. "Come with us, I'll sing you a song."

"Okay, that definitely sounded practiced," she breathed.

"I promise, I've never invited a woman to karaoke before." He pulled back just enough to ease out of her personal space, but his hand lingered on the back of her upper arm, and she was painfully aware of his fingertips brushing the side of her bra. Which didn't match her panties. Which shouldn't matter, but she had a sneaky suspicion if she accepted the invitation, it just might.

"My choice?" Evie's voice wavered as she realized she was seriously considering karaoke—and whatever else Liam was offering.

"For you, Evie, I'd sing just about anything." He chuckled and eased himself back against the bar.

She wobbled on her stool and took a steading breath. She needed a second to think this through…

"Tell you what." He glanced at his watch, a shiny thing that looked expensive and functional at the same time. "I'm going to get another round of drinks for my colleagues, so you've got some time to make up your mind. Finish your bellini and come up with a short list of tragic song choices."

"I might just head up to my room for a minute and change," she whispered. He glanced down at her skirt with appreciation, and she flushed.

"I hope you come back down." He brushed his fingertips over her knuckles as he stepped away from the bar, breaking that contact only when his body carried him too far away. "We're going to have fun tonight."

BUY WHEN THEY WEREN'T LOOKING TODAY!

AND CHASE GETS A BOOK, TOO!

NO TIME LIKE FOREVER (WARDHAM #6)

MARI Beadie used to love bartending weekday shifts at Danny's, Wardham's only pub. She could write lyrics between the lunch rush and the after dinner rush, and the night usually wrapped up relatively early.

That enjoyment had shifted to the past tense thanks to the far too regular—and far too grumpy—occupation of the barstool furthest from the door by Wardham's prodigal son, Chase Miller.

For one thing, there was no way she could write in front of him. For another, he attracted fans. And they weren't pint-buying fans either. Often they weren't even of legal drinking age.

But right now, she'd give her eyeteeth for Mr. Grumpy Pants to be in his seat at the end of the bar. So of course he was missing, probably out back taking yet another call from his girlfriend. He'd been getting lengthy calls from her a couple of times a week lately. Mari had finally put her foot down and insisted he take those calls outside when the pub was otherwise nice and quiet. She didn't need to hear all of his private business.

That was a stupid rule to enforce, because now it left her alone with her ex-boyfriend, Joel, who really didn't understand that they'd broken up.

He leaned over the bar, his floppy dark hair landing heavily in his eyes. She wanted to yell at him to get a haircut, but he'd just twist that into evidence that she cared.

Which she didn't. At all. The man—more of a boy, really—was a useless waste of space who tricked women into thinking he was hot stuff because he had a nice voice and looked good holding an electric guitar on stage.

He certainly didn't *play* the guitar. She might have been able to forgive the stupid haircut if he could play.

"Hey, baby girl," he crooned at her. His smile was lazy and knowing. Except he didn't know—that she hated that endearment with the passion of a thousand suns, for example. Or that she worked her butt off to support herself as a musician, and there was no way she'd date anyone who took the easy way out and lived at home so he could concentrate on his art. Particularly when his art seemed exclusively devoted to getting laid and looking hot.

Mari had moved off the family farm five years earlier, when she turned nineteen, and she wasn't going to fall for another guy who lived with his parents—no exceptions. "Joel, I'm not sure why you're here. We broke up."

He tsked at her and winked. Ick. "We just had a fight, Mari. It's how we are. I forgive you." Double ick. "I want to make it up to you. We've got a gig in London next weekend and I want you to come with me. We can even get a hotel room instead of driving back."

Which he'd want her to pay for, because he didn't have a credit card. Or a job. "Not interested."

"Don't be like that." He pulled a pick out of his pocket and started playing with it. Like he even needed a pick for the basic strumming he did while he sang songs written by people with actual talent.

"Let me guess, you'd love for us to play a couple of new songs, too. And when we're on stage, me shoved to the back corner, you'll announce them as *your* new songs and take the credit for writing them. No. Thank. You."

"I wouldn't do that to my girl." He cast a baleful look at her from under his bangs, as if he couldn't remember that she'd fallen for that trick in the winter and had told him never again. It didn't matter that song had been shitty, but it was the principle of the thing—something Joel seriously didn't get. "Maybe we could write a new song together."

Yep. Didn't get at all.

"I told you, I'm not your girl. In fact..." She cast around in her head for something that would convince him to leave her alone. "I'm seeing someone else."

He just stared at her, like the possibility of her having a real boyfriend who didn't use her for his own selfish advancement was so hard to believe.

She grinned. Ah ha! "Yes. That's right. I have a boyfriend. And he has short hair." That was a stupid thing to add, but she couldn't help herself.

Joel was too stupid for her to spend time with, but he wasn't brain dead. He saw right through her. It might have been the hair comment. She cursed herself and did a mental scan of her Facebook friends list. Who could she show him on her phone that he'd buy as her new beau?

"Oh, baby girl, playing hard to get is so unattractive."

If only him thinking of her as unattractive was enough to keep him away. "I'm not playing hard to get—seriously, Joel, I don't want you to get me!"

He settled in on a barstool and tapped at the smooth wood counter. "Sure you don't. Can I have a drink while you pretend to not want to write a song together?"

No way would he pay for it, but she poured him a weak gin and tonic anyway. Then she busied herself with straightening the tray of clean glasses under the bar.

Joel kept talking about the songs they could write together. She stopped listening—paying attention to Joel wasn't good for her blood pressure. "So tell me more about this boyfriend of yours," he finally said, a little louder than necessary. Had her ignoring act gotten under his skin? Good.

She straightened up and leaned against the bar, keeping a safe distance from his grabby hands. She wasn't scared of him, just annoyed, but she still didn't want him to touch her. She closed her eyes and pictured an imaginary boyfriend. The complete opposite of Joel. Curly hair with blond highlights. Strong. Big arms, washboard stomach, no tattoos. She liked tattoos on the right guy, but for the purposes of creating Joel's antithesis, they had to go. "He's a jock," she blurted out. "He plays all the sports. All of them. All the time."

Her ex smirked, as if to say *uh-huh*, but then his face fell.

"Everything okay, gorgeous?" The warm, rich voice rasped right behind her and she jumped what felt like six feet in the air. She spun around and slammed into a big, hard, warm, yummy-smelling chest. *Chase.* Oh sweet baby Jesus, what the hell was he doing? "Sorry I'm late. I was playing all the sports, all the time."

Mari couldn't process what was happening. It sounded like Chase was pretending to be her boyfriend. That was weird. He was also smiling. That was even weirder. He was standing really, really close to her. And he smelled amazing. "Uhm, Chase. Hi."

He crooked one eyebrow in a silent *are we gonna do this?* question. And for the life of her, she couldn't quite remember what *this* was, but she was all in. For doing anything with him, as long as he kept smiling and smelling like a surf god at the beach. When she didn't say anything else, he set his hands on her hips and turned her around. He didn't let go and she was pretty sure her insides were about to melt from joy. *What the hell was happening to her insides that they liked Chase Miller's touch?* "Mari? You going to introduce me to your friend?"

"Sure." Her voice shook, but Joel didn't seem to notice. He was staring at her very real imaginary boyfriend. "Joel Huggart, meet Chase Miller. Chase, Joel."

Chase shifted forward, keeping his left arm tightly banded around her waist, and offered his right hand to Joel. "Mari hasn't mentioned you, but then again, we haven't spent a lot of time talking about the past."

Joel took the hand, wincing as Chase squeezed a little too tightly. "We used to play together."

"Past tense?" Chase shifted his weight back on his heels, rocking Mari's body into his. Her back to his front. Wow, that felt good. She needed to put some space between them before she did something stupid like wiggle her hips like a heat-seeking missile. Mr. Grumpy Pants would soon make a return, and she didn't like him. She needed to remember that.

"Yes, past tense. Joel just popped in to say hi and then he'll be on his way, won't you?"

Her ex's face twisted in disappointment, but he nodded. Good, mission accomplished. She went to take a step away from Chase, but his arms tightened around her waist. She glanced back at him over her shoulder, not sure how she felt about the curious look on his face. She didn't hate it. Butterflies took flight in her stomach.

"Chase," she started to say, but after his name, her mind went blank.

"I have to…" His voice was unexpectedly gruff, and he tried again. "I actually have to go. I just wanted to see you for a minute. And I'll be back later."

"Okay," she whispered, not sure what he was doing, but it seemed like a decent way out of their charade. But then he turned her around and ever so slowly lowered his mouth to hers.

This wasn't a kiss for show. It was tentative and exploratory, like he wasn't sure he knew what to do. As if it had been a while since he'd done this. But kissing was like riding a bike, and holy crap, could Chase ride a bike. After the first few moments, commanding lust took over and he hauled her against his body. Her lips parted in invitation and he took all she was offering and more. The press of his tongue against hers made her whimper and wiggle closer, and when he pulled back she chased his face for a last little nibble of his lower lip. At some point she'd wrapped her hands around his neck and the short curls at his nape felt like magic against her fingertips.

He stared at her for a moment, and slowly she dropped back into reality. Her lips were swollen, her nipples were hard, and she'd practically begged Chase Miller to keep kissing her. She dropped her arms as her face turned red.

READ NO TIME LIKE FOREVER TODAY!

ACKNOWLEDGEMENTS

AKA THE PEOPLE WHO WARM MY SOUL

I usually start my acknowledgements with a nod to my husband, but since I dedicated this book to him, we can move right to my usual crew of cheerleaders: Rachel, Natalie, Hannah, Andraena, and Lori, whose collective positivity could power the sun. I'm humbled by your faith and support.

My sister, who hates reading, and my mother-in-law, who hates reading anything that doesn't feature dwarves or dragons, and yet they both scoured the book for typos and inconsistencies. The best, and most unlikely, proofreading crew a girl could have.

Molly and Jennifer, who don't pull any punches and push me to be a better writer. Any remaining repetition and pathetic use of crutch words is on me and my stubbornness.

Facebook, and all of the awesome people who have liked my page, promoted my books, sent new fans my way, shared lovely messages, and so on…I'm late to the game, but I get it now, and I'm grateful for the direct connection to readers.

Book bloggers! I try to keep an updated list of these amazing friends on my website.

And finally, the Divas, without whom I'd still be stumbling around with a sheaf of papers and a crayon sketch of a cover.

Their collective wisdom is staggering, and surpassed only by their collective kindness.

ABOUT THE AUTHOR

Zoe York lives in London, Ontario with her young family. She's currently chugging Americanos, wiping sticky fingers, and dreaming of heroes in and out of uniform.

Connect with Zoe:
www.zoeyork.com
zoeyorkwrites@gmail.com

BE A WARDHAM AMBASSADOR

I'd love to have you join my Facebook reader group! Click on the link, or search "Wardham Ambassadors" on Facebook.

https://www.facebook.com/groups/WardhamAmbassadors/

www.ingramcontent.com/pod-product-compliance
Lightning Source LLC
Chambersburg PA
CBHW050850190726

48286CB00007B/2315